Emma Lathen

Murder Makes the Wheels Go Round Screenplay

"Thatcher is Nero Wolfe with portfolio"
"The American Agatha Christie"
"New York Times Book Reviews"

Simply Media Inc.
POB 481
Lincoln, MA 01773-0481
www.simplymedia.com

simplymedia® is a trademark of Simply Media Inc.

Copyright© 2017 by Deaver Brown for the Cover, Preface & Introduction.

Copyright© 2017 by Emma Lathen, Martha Henissart, Simply Media & Deaver Brown for the text.

This is a work of fiction with all characters and incidents fictional.

SimplyMedia®
Making Learning Easy

Murder Makes the Wheels Go Round
4th of 37 Emma Lathen Mysteries

Reviews

"Probably the best living American writer of detective stories."

C. P. Snow

"Emma Lathen writes permanent classics in the detective field. No superlatives are adequate."

The New York Times

"The writing is really first class—a continual delight."

The Times Literary Supplement

"Mystery writing at its very finest."

St. Louis Post-Dispatch

"First-rate mystery, ably plotted and beautifully written."

Los Angeles Times

"Unusual style and ingenuity. The best of its kind."

The New Yorker

"The financial involutions of an unusual trust are clearly and absorbingly presented and the murder puzzle is sound and well-clued. A find."

The New York Times Book Review

"Emma Lathen—what more need one say to assure a best of the year in detecting?"

Newsweek

"She is peerless in style, wit, inventively credible plotting, and character bits."

Los Angeles Times

"Emma Lathen uses her good wit to make banks and accounting companies an exciting background for big-business deviltry. The best successful female writer in this field."

Chicago Tribune

"Emma Lathen is the most intriguing mystery-writer in our country in at over a decade."

Dorothy B. Hughes

"John Putnam Thatcher is one of the very few important series of detectives to enter the field—a completely civilized and urbane man, whose charm is as remarkable as his acumen."

Anthony Boucher

Murder Makes the Wheels Go Round

"Imperturbable banker John Putnam Thatcher . . . will have to deal with financial shenanigans, geopolitical unrest, and somebody even more eager to make a killing on the deal."

Kirkus Reviews

"Lathen's long-running series . . . is notable for its combination of murder and the arcane mysteries of high finance."

Publishers Weekly

"Another great Thatcher novel. . . . Refreshing. . . .
Well-written. . . . Thatcher is a great character.

Midwest Book Review

Murder also happens to the rich and mighty, just ask Emma Lathen!

The New York Times Book Review calls her "urbane, witty, faultless, delightful." She provides suspense with fascinating insights into businesses and the lives of the rich and powerful. From International to local businesses, where danger and intelligence go hand-in-hand.

"Emma Lathen writes permanent classics in the detective field. No superlatives are adequate." The New York Times

"The writing is really first class—a continual delight."
Times Literary Supplement

"Mystery writing at its very finest."
St. Louis Post-Dispatch

"First-rate mystery, ably plotted and beautifully written. She is peerless in style, wit, inventively credible plotting, and character bits."
LA Times

"Unusual style and ingenuity. The best of its kind."
The New Yorker

"The financial involutions of an unusual trust are clearly and absorbingly presented and the murder puzzle is sound and well-clued. A find."
The New York Times Book Review

"Emma Lathen—what more need one say to assure a best of the year in detecting?"
Newsweek

"She is peerless in style, wit, inventively credible plotting, and character bits."
Los Angeles Times

"Emma Lathen uses her good wit to make banks, and accounting companies an exciting background for big-business deviltry, and become the best successful female writer in this field."
Chicago Tribune

Murder also happens to the rich and mighty, just ask Emma Lathen!

The New York Times Book Review calls her "urbane, witty, faultless, delightful." She provides suspense with fascinating insights into businesses and the lives of the rich and powerful. From International to local businesses, where danger and intelligence go hand-in-hand.

24 John Putnam Thatcher
Emma Lathen Mysteries

1. Banking on Death 1961. Manufacturing basics.
2. A Place for Murder 1963. Old Rich v Town's People.
3. Accounting for Murder 1964. Accounting.
4. Murder Makes the Wheels Go Round 1966. Cars.
5. Death Shall Overcome 1966. Integration & Civil Rights.
6. Murder Against the Grain 1967. Options Trading.
7. A Stitch in Time 1968. Health Care.
8. Come to Dust 1968. Fund Raising.
9. When in Greece 1969. International Business.
10. Murder to Go 1969. Fast Food.
11. Pick Up Sticks 1970. Second Home Developments.
12. Ashes to Ashes 1971. Real Estate Development.
13. The Longer the Thread 1971. Cut & Sew Off Shore
14. Murder Without Icing 1972. Professional Sports.
15. Sweet and Low 1974. Candy Bars & Consumer.
16. By Hook or by Crook 1975. Antique Rugs.
17. Double, Double, Oil and Trouble 1978. Oil.
18. Going for the Gold 1981. Olympics/Amateur Sport.
19. Green Grow the Dollars 1982. Mail Order/Nursery.
20. Something in the Air 1988. Discount Airlines.
21. East is East 1991. International, Robotics & Finance.
22. Right on the Money 1993. Mergers & Acquisitions.
23. Brewing Up a Storm 1996. Beer.
24. A Shark Out of Water 1997. Government Projects.

6 Elizabeth & John Putnam Thatcher
Emma Lathen Mysteries

John Putnam Thatcher reorganizes the Sloan, becomes Chairman, Charlie Trinkam President, Ken Nicolls SVP, Elizabeth Thatcher Head of IT & Venture Capital, Walter Bowman VP of Yes, Everett Gabler VP of No & Maria Corsa, Miss Corsa's niece, a direct report to Elizabeth Thatcher. George Lancer, former Chairman, Brad Withers, former President & Miss Corsa are retired but curious.

The Sloan has automated its branches, moved Corporate Headquarters to Ireland, set up IT in India, established the VC division in Ireland & Austin, and sold off the Sloan Headquarters building in New York City. The Sloan has gone private with the above active individuals being the major shareholders and become the largest Bank in the World by Capital value.

25. Political Murder 1999. Death of a Senator.
26. Dot Com Murder 2001. Death of a Dot Com Leader.
27. Biking Murder 2005. Death of a Bike Lane Advocate.
28. Nonprofit Murder 2008. Death of a Nonprofit CEO.
29. Union Murder 2010. Death of a Union Leader.
30. Gig Murder: 2016. Death of a Gig Litigant.

Preface

Henissart and Latsis attended Harvard graduate school back in the day. Henissart attended and graduated from Harvard Law School. Latsis received a PHD in Economics.

At first they were friends and then roommates. Latsis worked in the CIA after graduation. She spent two years in Rome employed by the UN's Food and Agricultural Organization before returning to Wellesley College to teach Economics. Henissart went to New York to practice law.

In 1960 Henissart took a corporate legal job at Raytheon in Boston. She stayed with Latsis during her house hunt. She asked what good mysteries were around and was told there weren't any left.

They then said, "Let's write one." With that they were off and running in their lifetime entrepreneurial writing venture. This reminded me of my old friend Alex Goodwin, now Levitch, the only man I know who has ever changed his last name not to his wife's, bringing me the Umbroller type stroller as a business project and I said, "Let's do it." We did. We were Choate roommates and had gone our separate ways until we had our first taste of organization life for me at General Foods and Alex in law at the US Justice Dept. in DC.

Latsis and Henissart had an unusual relationship for writers but not for entrepreneurial partners. They began each book by first agreeing on the basic structure and major characters; then they wrote alternating chapters. Latsis then composed the first complete draft on yellow pads and produced this edition for Henissart to review. Henissart then typed out the final draft.

They would then get together for a final joint rewrite, eliminate inconsistencies, and synthesize the work into a coherent whole. Unlike the tradition of a Hemingway and Fitzgerald with an editor like Max Perkins, they jointly did their own editorial work as equal partners in their enterprise.

Most mystery buffs have had that moment of running out of acceptable books to read. Each of us can remember vividly the wonderful time when we found another series to read. This can be your moment with the Emma Lathen series!

I can remember the time I learned about Agatha Christie, Thomas Perry, Dick Francis, and Emma Lathen herself. Some writers tap out and get off track like Patricia Cornwell. But they are often terrific while on track.

Being practical as well as talented people, Henissart and Latsis took up the challenge and wrote 31 books together before Latsis died in 1997.

24 were Emma Lathen John Thatcher books and 7 Ben Stafford political works written under the name R. G. Dominic. As good entrepreneurs, they let the Stafford series go when the John Thatcher series outsold it by a substantial amount.

The series has been extended to six more featuring Thatcher's daughter, Elizabeth, and most of the rest of the cast, this time moving Thatcher up to Chairman, Trinkam President, Nicolls SVP, Elizabeth Head of IT & VC, Bowman VP of Yes, Gabler VP of No, and Miss Corsa's niece on board working for Elizabeth. Lancer, Withers, and Rose Corsa have retired but remain shareholders and are curious as well.

There will be more as The Sloan adapts to the modern world by having moved their HQ to Ireland in a tax inversion, automating its branches to be more mobile and less subject to regulation, centering IT in India, venture capital in Austin, going private, and becoming the largest bank in the world measured by capital value.

Emma Lathen used Wall Street, banking, and business as the backdrop for her inspiration for a series of entertaining mysteries. The New York Times said, "John Putnam Thatcher is Nero Wolfe with portfolio." In fact many readers turn to Lathen when they have finished the Nero Wolfe stories. Another New York Times reviewer said, "Emma Lathen is the American Agatha Christie."

The Daily News said Emma Lathen was "The Agatha Christie of Wall Street."

Their seemingly infallible instincts helped them recognize that business people were big mystery readers and could afford to buy a series, exactly what my Aunt Dorothy did, who had introduced me to Emma Lathen. Both understood business seemingly totally, sympathizing with its practitioners and advisors, since Henissart was Chief Legal Counsel at Raytheon, then the largest high tech company in Massachusetts, and Latsis a Harvard Economics PHD and Professor of Economics at Wellesley.

They created the name Emma Lathen out of a combination of letters in their own names, something they had great fun doing. M of Mary and Ma of Martha, and Lat of Latsis and Hen of Henissart. This was reinforced by Emma from Jane Austen. And viola--Emma Lathen was born!

No one troubled to find out who Emma Lathen was for years. The authors kept it quiet to protect Henissart's clients from possible embarrassment.

They created an ensemble of characters to enrich their stories and carry people's knowledge about the Thatcher group from book to book, much like Agatha did to a more limited extent with Hastings and Jap joining Poirot in many books. Emma Lathen anticipated TV series such asPerry Mason, Mary Tyler Moore, and later Friends that created a cast of characters so we knew them from the beginning of each story and didn't have to labor to learn a new group.

Pure whipped cream without the calories.

Introduction

Emma Lathen used Wall Street, banking, and business as the backdrop for her inspiration for a series of entertaining mysteries. The New York Times said, "John Putnam Thatcher is Nero Wolfe with portfolio." In fact many readers turn to Lathen when they have finished the Nero Wolfe stories. Another New York Times reviewer said, "Emma Lathen is the American Agatha Christie."

An LA review from the Daily News said, "The Agatha Christie of Wall Street."

With those accolades she surely deserves our respect. More personally, she is worthy of reading, especially after you have run out of Wolfe and Christie mysteries.

What is most charming about this 24 book series is that her entourage is in all the books, much like successful TV series such as Friends. Rex Stout had a similar group but they didn't appear in every mystery. Agatha Christie had Captain Hastings, Miss Lemon, and Japp who appeared together occasionally; the TV series got them into more episodes to the delight of Agatha fans.

I was personally introduced to Lathen by my Aunt Dorothy who was a business woman back in the day building houses in Minneapolis and then in World War II moving on to Seattle with her husband to do so. Interestingly, this is the only author my Aunt ever recommended. I have been forever grateful to her for doing so. Much like a Lathen character, my Aunt knew what money was good for and what it wasn't. Uncle Chester and she built houses in the warm six months in Minneapolis and later Seattle with their building boom in World War II, and then took off the other six to enjoy worldwide cruises for the rest of the year.

Her postcards let me follow her from country to country, place to place, as they had a grand old time of it. She was introduced to Lathen in a ship's library with their books bound in lovely yellow sturdy boards produced by Lathen's English publisher. It all seemed to fit; English like Christie; on ship; with business people who could relate to Lathen and her cast of characters.

Emma Lathen was the pseudonym for Martha Henissart and Mary Jane Latsis who wrote 24 adeptly structured detective stories featuring a banker, John Putnam Thatcher, and crack amateur sleuth much like Jane Marple. Thatcher is every bit as endearing and interesting as Poirot and Marple, Nero Wolfe and Archie, and Sue Grafton's Kinsey Millhone, Henry, and company.

Each story starts out with a business/banking motif, points to motives other than money, and winds up with money not emotions being the clue to the solution. Thatcher's clear headed knowledge of money, banking, business, and human foibles is as only bankers can know, leads to his eureka moments, which are always fabulously turned out.

Thatcher's purpose is curiosity coupled with a desire to get his loans and the bank's investments repaid which leads to his identifying killers and delivering them over to the police.

Why was banking used as a backdrop for these mysteries? Henissart and Latsis put it best, "There is nothing on Lord's earth a banker can't get into." Voila, and much like their rapier like insights and wits of these charming tough minded authors.

Thatcher was the first fictional detective to come out of the world of business and finance. He became an instant hit on Wall Street and beyond in business and financial circles. This makes him perfect for today's millennial and Z generations so enthusiastic about entrepreneurial life in education, nonprofits, and commercial life, all of which are represented in the work of Emma Lathen.

Martha Henissart chucked when telling me their best bookstore was on Wall Street itself.

Pure whipped cream without the calories.

Cast

Regulars

John Putnam Thatcher, Senior Vice President of the Sloan, the Third Largest Bank in the World.

Charlie Trinkam, Thatcher's Second in Command in the Trust Department.

Everett Gabler, the informal VP of No, who identifies the weaknesses in every situation.

Walter Bowman, the informal VP of Yes, who advocates new investment opportunities as the Head of the Sloan Research Department.

Ken Nicolls, the budding young banker who operates as an assistant for Thatcher, Trinkam, or Gabler, depending on the circumstance. Jane Schneider Nicolls, his wife.

Miss Rose Corsa, Thatcher's secretary, efficient, and generally unflappable.

Tom Robichaux, Investment Banker/promoter, much married, a bon vivant, with conservative proper Quaker Devane as his partner, in the Robichaux & Devane multigeneration boutique investment bank. Thatcher's Harvard College Roommate back in the day, who makes money.

George Charles Lancer, Stately Chairman of the Sloan Board of Directors.

Lucy Lancer, the perceptive witty wife of George.

Brad Withers, World Traveler, Sloan President, outside Ambassador, and the nominal boss of John Putnam Thatcher. Husband of Carrie Withers, perceptive upright Yankee lady.

Stanton Carruthers, Sloan lawyer.

Elizabeth ("Becky") Thatcher, John Putnam Thatcher's second daughter, stunning, smart, and much like his abolitionist grandmother. VP of IT & VC investments.

Occasional Characters

Professor Cardwell ("Cardy") Carlson, the father-in-law of Laura, Thatcher's oldest daughter. An erudite impractical professor.

Mrs. Agnes Carlson, Laura's mother-in-law who keeps Ben in line and up to form.

Dr. Ben Carlson, Thatcher's son-in-law and Laura's husband. Stays quietly in the background.

Laura Thatcher Carlson, Thatcher's first daughter & family organizer.

Jack Thatcher, youngest of the Thatcher children and much like Tom Robichaux and hence now the junior partner in the firm of Robichaux, Devane & Thatcher..

Sam, Sloan Chauffer known for prompt service, comforting wit, and a warming temperament.

Sheldon, Office boy known for moving equipment, getting Bromo Seltzer for hung over trust officers, and doing other small nefarious chores.

Billings, the sardonic respectful elevator operator known for succinct observations about the day's goings on.

Don Trotman, the Devonshire Doorman and Jack of all Trades onsite.

Albert Nelson, John Putnam Thatcher's man servant and general helper.

Francis Devane, Quaker partner of Tom Robichaux in Robichaux & Devane, later Robichaux, Devane & Thatcher when Jack Thatcher, John's son, became a name partner.

Arnie Berman, Waymark-Sims seasoned cigar chomping investment pro.

Claire Todd, Ken Nicolls secretary.

Miss Prettyman, Brad Withers secretary.

Characters only in *Murder Makes the Wheels Go Round Screenplay*

Michigan Motors Monarchs of the Road

Plantagenet: The Crown Jewel of Motoring

    Scepter: Symbol of Achievement
    Royale: The Executive Car without Peer

Lancaster: Beauty Bred to Service

    Majestic: The First Family Car
    Viscount: Elegance in Driving
    Victory: Flagship of Convertibles
    Chancellor: The Thoroughbred of Station Wagons

Buccaneer: The Sea Dogs of the Michigan Fleet

    Drake: The Lively Fun Loving Compact
    Howard: Compact Economy with Big Car Comfort.

Raleigh: The Cavalier Convertible

Hotspur: The Golden Sports Car

Arnie Berman, representative of stock underwriter, Waymark-Sims.

Frank Krebbel, the new MM president.

Stu Eberhart, former MM President.

Lionel French, MM Chairman.

Ray Jensen, one of the three jailed executives. Former head of MM's big Plantagenet Division & had had the inside rail to get the Presidency.

Buck Holzinger, second of the three jailed executives & creator of the Drake. Wife Diane is part of a rich meatpacking company family centered in Chicago.

Orin Dunn, third of the three Jailed Executives, and the junior member of the team.

Ed Wahl, who takes over for Jensen when Jensen is jailed. Wife Audrey is a drinker and troublemaker.

Celia Jensen, estranged wife of Ray & primed to marry Glen Madsen, MM economist.

Louise Burns, Celia's helpful sister and her helpful husband, Father Larry Burns.

Glen Madsen, MM economist tapped early as the prospective murderer.

Mack, the MM chauffeur who drives Thatcher everywhere.

Captain Georgeson, State Policeman in charge of the murder investigationMack

Fabian X Riley, DOJ investigator & in love with MM executive secretary Susan Price.

Susan Price, MM executive secretary and attached to Riley.

Lincoln Hauser, MM PR man that used to be with the Sloan and Thatcher relieved he is no longer.

Julian Summers, Riley's boss.

Emma Lathen Political Mysteries

Emma Lathen: As R. B. Dominic

1. Murder Sunny Side Up 1968. Agriculture.
2. Murder in High Place 1969. Overseas Travelers.
3. There is No Justice 1971. Supreme Court.
4. Epitaph for a Lobbyist 1974. Lobbyists.
5. Murder Out of Commission 1976. Nuke Plants.
6. The Attending Physician 1980. Health Care.
7. Unexpected Developments 1983. Military.

Tom Walker Mysteries
Patricia Highsmith Style
Deaver Brown, Author

01. 18. Football & Superbowl.
02. Abduct. Sexual Misconduct.
03. Body. Planned Eliminations for Money.
04. Comfortable. Avoiding Consequences.
05. Death. Wrong Place at the Wrong Time.
06. Enthusiast. Opportunity Murder.
07. Fraud. Taking Your Chances.
08. Greed. Heirs Who Know Better.
09. Heat. Heir Arrogance.
10. Prodigy. Tom Walker's First Case.

A similarly popular Simply Media mystery series.

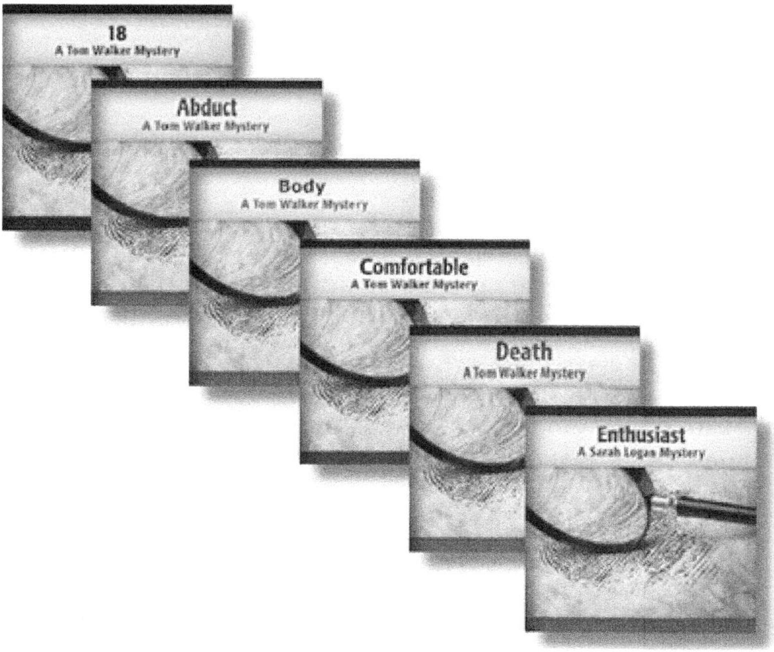
18
A Tom Walker Mystery
Abduct
A Tom Walker Mystery
Body
A Tom Walker Mystery
Comfortable
A Tom Walker Mystery
Death
A Tom Walker Mystery
Enthusiast
A Sarah Logan Mystery

Financial & Other Facts

Emma Lathen is all about the money not the emotion. In that light:

1. To provide financial incentives for collectors, Simply Media and others savings on groups of 6 eBooks, and the SuperSku (learning from the Star Wars franchise) "all in" collection.

2. Trust that we have all enjoyed this. But as Willie Nelson, Oscar Wilde, and others have said, we aren't above the money. Stay well. And thanks from all of us on the Emma Lathen team.

Deaver Brown, Publisher & Editor.
www.simplymedia.com

SimplyMedia®
Making Learning Easy

Murder Makes the Wheels Go Round Screenplay

4th Emma Lathen Mystery

Ext. Sloan Building-Day

Establishing shot. New York headquarters for the Sloan Guaranty Trust. A modern banking headquarters building, glass, and metal dominates. Use shot from Banking on Death.

John Putnam Thatcher (70, handsome, quietly sharp, smart & shrewd), a Wall Street Banker, wears conservative casual business casual attire, and an ironic expression. Everett Gabler (68+, fussy, picky, sharp & usually right) is a long time employee of the Sloan and the cautious VP who finds all the difficulties.

The office is comfortable and somewhat spare with traditional mahogany furniture. No trophies, photos, or clutter. Wide windows. Beyond his office door is Assistant/secretary Miss Corsa's (35, formidable, seems older, a stickler) outside room.

Scene 1-Int.-Investment Committee Meeting Room-Day

Bowman (55, large, jovial, astute, quick on his feet): John, glad to catch you in here; you should stay for this week's investment committee meeting starting in just 10 minutes. I know you like your *ex officio member* status to be *in absentia* . But you should make an exception this week.

With that, he pops out. Thatcher looks wary and impaled.

Just then the door opens with Charlie Trinkam (45 year handsome woman, 2nd in command of the Trust Dept), ushering in Hugh Waymark (80, shrewd, quick), exuding enthusiasm, and one of his associates, Arnold Berman (40s, rotund backroom person).

Thatcher: At least you look doleful, Arnie. I feel poleaxed to be here by Withers, Bowman, and others. So I wouldn't want your good efforts to go to waste, so I'll stay.

Waymark: Now John, I came in person because this investment will be the most profitable in our firm's history. Our people and yours are sold on it.

Trinkam: Walter I note your rapt absorption in your papers on the table, something challenging must be afoot.

Bowman reacts slightly. Waymark cuts off Trinkam's irony.

Waymark: We're thinking of offering three million five of the common. If the market holds up, we should get at least $55 for them. Of course we haven't worked out the fine print.

This meant Waymark-Sims would sell 3.5 million shares at $55 each, give the proceeds to the company, hand over the shares, get their profit, and turnover the shares to the customers.. First though, they needed other underwriters like the Sloan to help sell all the shares and complete the offer.

Trinkam: Hugh, since Bowman's not looking at me, and you didn't tell us what you are selling, it will be fascinating to hear what you are trying to rope us into. I have my seat belt on.

Thatcher: Hugh, I have a mild interest in hearing more. When you shroud your pitch, my worst fears are often confirmed. Only the spine-chilling particulars from you remain to be heard.

Hugh smiles, takes a deep breath, and plunges in.

Waymark: Michigan Motors. That's what we are talking about. And this is going to be big. Out in Detroit the Big Three is a thing of the past. It's going to be the Big Four soon, with MM right up there with the others. Here, look at these figures.

There was a substantial pause, broken by Thatcher.

Thatcher: Now let's see. Exactly when was Michigan Motors convicted of rigging government bids and price fixing?

Assuming the question to be rhetorical, no one replies.

I seem to recall that it was last October, wasn't it? The largest antitrust case in American History, as I recall.

Headlines like:

Auto conspiracy charged by govt; Multibillion dollar price fixing of cars. Rigged bids in defense contracts; 9 auto execs go on trial.

And resulting in:

Govt produces records of March 15 plotting; Car conspirators guilty; 9 auto execs get 6 months in jail. As you can hear, I paid attention.

Trinkam: Yes, John, it was October. I was just coming back from Toronto when the government produced photocopies of that meeting in March, remember Walter?

Bowman plaintively.

Bowman: I remember.

Hugh Waymark gamely steps in.

Waymark: Of course I don't deny that the trial was important. But what's past is past. MM has a great future.

Trinkam: That's just it, Hugh. Is it past? MM was the ringleader of the whole price fixing plot, after all. Don't you remember?

Hugh opens his mouth to retort but Charlie continues.

Trinkam: And even worse, the tip-off to the Justice Department came from inside MM.

Charlie pauses for effect.

That's a company with a past. But I'm not so sure about the future. They broke the law, they got caught, just like the others. But MM has an inside informer willing to pull the rug out from under them.

John says grimly.

Thatcher: Nicely put, Charlie.

Hugh reels off tons of data to try to swamp the objections. Charlie clearly has adopted a rollicking view of the goings on and the Sloan's possible involvement.

Charlie: What did shakeups include at MM? I can see Arnie has reason to be dour like John.

Hugh glanced at his associate. Obediently Berman, who had been balefully studying his cigar, hitched himself forward and spoke. It was not with Hugh's vigor but with a mild philosophical skepticism, more in tune with John and Charlie's perspective.

Arnie Berman: Thanks for the lead in, Charlie.

This cut the ice as Arnie clearly knows how to do.

There's a new president; a capable competent accountant, Frank Krebbel. He was formerly the controller who had nothing to do with the price fixing. He has a good head on his shoulders.

Berman sat down to smiles from the Sloan people.

Trinkam: That was mercifully short, Arnie. Now who was the former president? Oh yes, Eberhart. Did they get him on the antitrust violations?

Berman: They couldn't prove a thing. But he had to resign. The Judge did not say good things about him.

Hugh tries to speak again; Charlie beats him to the punch.

Trinkam: Is this new president the extent of the management shakeup?

Hugh launches into accolades again but slows down and stops. Signals Arnie who starts up.

Berman: MM has three people in jail, just like the other two firms involved, the Head of Plantagenet, his assistant, and one more.

Trinkam: Wasn't the Head supposedly the brains behind the deal?

Berman nods.

Berman: Ray Jensen. One of the real whiz kids of the industry. He set up the March 15th meeting.

Waymark impatiently.

Waymark: Yes, yes.

Even Waymark sees Berman has their attention. So stops.

Berman: Jensen went to jail along with his assistant, a kid called Dunn. The other MM man in the clink is Buck Holzinger, who ran the Buccaneer line of compacts. They have been in jail since October; a couple of other division managers had to resign. Not enough evidence to indict them, but enough to suspect. I suppose you could call that a sweeping management turnover.

Thatcher: A shade too careful. Does that mean Jensen and Holzinger are out of the company for good or just for the duration of their sentences?

There was another long silence.

Berman: That hasn't been decided yet.

Waymark: They were fired. They're both out of the company for good.

Berman corrects his boss gently.

Berman: At the other companies the big boys who went to jail got the bounce. But MM hasn't announced their decisions yet. That has raised a lot of talk.

Trinkham: I guess it has. And things must be just dandy for the guys running Plantagenet and Buccaneer now. I have to hand it to you, Hugh. You've got a beaut on your hands. All of this and an unidentified informer too.

Waymark: Now, now. Just because a public announcement hasn't been made doesn't mean there isn't a clear policy in the front office. I assure you that out at MM the difficulties associated with the trial are over. That includes the informant.

Bowman: Hugh is absolutely right. The antitrust trial and convictions are history now. Let's forget about price fixing and just look at these earnings' estimates. MM is a good buy.

Thatcher: Thank you for your thoughts. I am off to my next appointment. Let me know how things work out.

He flees.

Scene 2-Int.-Thatcher's Office-Day

Thatcher: Miss Corsa, I don't want to be disturbed for the rest of the day, especially by Walter Bowman. Are you prepared to do some stealing for me?

Miss Corsa shows her disdain for his little jokes, highlighted by her chaste bunch of blue violets for Easter and her efficient navy blue dress. She waits patiently for more.

I want you to get the Michigan Motors file from Research before Bowman and his people have a chance to doctor it.

Miss Corsa: Oh, they wouldn't do that, Mr. Thatcher.

Her tone was reproving as it often was when he made one of his little jokes.

Thatcher: They have done it to me before, Miss Corsa. I have complete confidence in your ability to abstract the files from Research before the meeting ends upstairs and a similar respect for Walter's capacity to submerge any material unfavorable to the company he is trying to sell to the Investment Committee.

Pause. Miss Corsa walks out and back in.

You see Miss Corsa, supremely indifferent that you may be to the substance, you have produced a bulging folder within twenty minutes. Bring your pad in.

She does. Thatcher starts to read.

Ah ha, Bowman wouldn't have let a lot of this survive. You saved it, Miss Corsa.

She taps her pencil on the pad meaningfully as she lifts an eyebrow.

Alright, alright. I'll start. The contents are in rough chronological order; first, September articles describing rumors of a gigantic antitrust case in the offing, then the bombshell with its screaming October headlines. Thumbnail profiles of the defendants, MM's Ray Jensen was the "lantern jawed hard-nosed boss" of the Plantagenet Division, Buck Holzinger was "the glad hander from Buccaneer," and Orin Dunn was the "pale but composed" member of the team, and then on to the summing up from the bench. Events unfolded largely as remembered. The DOJ had struck in October, charging MM with price fixing and rigged bids. Detroit had countered with a nolo plea or not accepting or denying responsibility but agreeing to accept punishment.

At this point in the MM saga the party started to get livelier. The US Solicitor General appeared in Court in person; the nolo plea, which could have saved the auto industry untold millions in treble damages was rejected by the DOJ. Detroit muttered resentfully about vindictive public officials in high places, insiders said the DOJ must have a sure thing, and something else happened.

Overnight fifty million Americans suddenly realized what this legal palaver about artificially maintained prices meant for them, that they might have been suckered into paying more for last year's car than they otherwise would have. Avidly an outraged public read about bids to the government, price collusion, bellboys who had borne refreshments to price fixers, and finally about what even the *Wall Street Journal* called "a prosecution blockbuster" with copies of Ray Jensen's handwritten notes covering the March 15 meeting, including a detailed explanation of the famous code system used by the conspirators to exchange price information and allocate government contracts.

The court decision was a foregone conclusion. The next set of clippings, with photographs, showed the convicted felons, including a scowling Jensen and Holzinger, with his jocularity impaired, being led behind prison bars. Then came a playful account of Christmas gifts from the UAW to the imprisoned: gift-wrapped *Monopoly* sets. Thereafter the press coverage had abated until early April when Bowman's research hit another covey of clippings.

Early retirement for Muldoon. McKay off payroll, prexy announces Blakesly to relocate.

They added up to a clean sweep of the executive conspirators by seemingly virtuous corporations with the exception of MM. The firms involved proclaimed: (1) they had not known their employees were violating the Sherman Antitrust Act, the Clayton Act, or even local parking ordinances, (2) they could not countenance such malefactions.

    John smiles.

The judge's tart observations when the ex-president of MM, Stuart Eberhart, had delivered himself of similar sentiments in the courtroom were not supportive of MM.

Charlie was right. MM did not emerge happily from the great price fixing conspiracy, if indeed it has emerged at all.

    He continues dictating.

Turning over several woolly-headed statements on Ethics in Business by pastors, educators, and other social commentators, John finally came across a suggestive small item: Speculation is Rife at MM. Industry sources are buzzing with questions about the future of Ray Jensen and Buck Holzinger at MM. MM is keeping its plans to itself.

Thank you Miss Corsa. Type it up as quickly as possible after you return the files.

    She leaves.

Thatcher out loud: They are probably still sorting through the numbers at the meeting upstairs, with volleys back and forth across the financial net. But, until we know who tipped off the DOJ to the conspiracy, and we learn what MM planned to do with its erring executives, the projections are not sound enough for a Sloan investment.

Scene 3-Int.-Frank Krebbel's Office-Day

Frank Krebbel (President MM, 60, trim, executive looking): Lionel, we have to make some sort of announcement if we want to go ahead with a new issue, you know.

Chairman Lionel French (70, elegant, cautious, no fool) speaks with a ponderous air of regret.

Lionel French : It is a shame to rake the whole thing up again.

Krebbel: Lionel, I have spent months pulling MM through a bad time. Now sales and production are flowing again. Cars are selling; buyers are excited; record results are expected. The forthcoming union negotiations and dealing with the jailed executives are the only serious issues we have.

In short, we should make some sort of announcement. It is a shame. We've put this off too long. It does us no good to leave this unsettled, particularly when trying to raise capital.

French: Darn unfair. All this trouble because some secretary went running to the DOJ.

Krebbel: It wasn't a secretary, Lionel. It was someone with Ray's notes, someone who knew all about all the meetings. Someone at a high executive level.

French: For goodness sake, leave it alone.

Krebbel: Well then what about an announcement?

The Chairman frowned and pursed his lips.

French: Look Frank, perhaps we should come to some arrangement with Ray when he gets out. He's very, ah, informed about the company. And he did go to jail without telling the government anything they didn't already know. Do you think Ray is likely to make trouble if we fire him now?

Krebbel: He'll try.

French shook his head and went on.

French: Then take Buck. You never can tell what he'll come up with. After all he did develop the Drake.

Krebbel: As you say it doesn't pay to underestimate Buck.

French: That's just it. I tell you Frank, we are going to have to hold up the announcement. The board will need more time to...think things through.

Krebbel looks at French without sympathy. He nods.

French: You know Jensen can be difficult. You don't suppose he might be tempted to go back to the DOJ with information to implicate Stuart or anyone else?

Krebbel: Let him.

French leaves.

Scene 4 -Int.-Ray Jensen's Old Office at MM-Day

Ray Jensen(45, executive): Knocks and walks in.

Ray Jensen: I want to thank you personally, Ed.

Ed Wahl (45, rough & ready manager): What for?

Jensen: Why for minding the store while I was gone. Just talked to Krebbel; gave me my old job back.

Jensen leaves.

Scene 5 -Int.-Orin Dunn's Living Room-Day

Orin walks in.

His wife (30ish, positive, pretty, nice): So nice to have you back, Orin. You'll get your job back and everything will be fine again.

Orin (35, tired Executive type): Look, can't you understand? What if they don't take me back? I'm too young to be a has been.

Scene 6 -Int.-Buck Holzinger's Living Room-Day

Buck walks in.

Diane Holzinger (45, looks 35, beautiful shrewd woman): You're going to have to fight to get back into the company.

Buck Holzinger: (45, handsome, funny, successful): It we are going to face facts we might as well face the fact that I'm through. It's hard but there it is, I like the new fence.

Diane Holzinger: MM has announced nothing. There's a lot of talk they'll take Ray back.

Buck admiring his living room with undisguised pleasure.

Buck Holzinger: So?

Diane Holzinger: You're not going to take that lying down. Orin and you will have to spike his guns. There's nothing Ray would like better than keep you out in the cold.

Buck Holzinger: Not much I can do about it. Good to see the old place.

>Di gripped her purse with white knuckles.

Diane Holzinger: It is Krebbel who counts now. Ray's probably already gone up to see him by now. You have to do something about it, Buck.

Buck Holzinger: It means a lot to you doesn't it, Di?

Diane Holzinger: Yes it does.

Buck Holzinger: OK then. For you.

>His captivating grin and gets Di to smile back.

Scene 7 -Int.-Thatcher's Office-Day

>Thatcher walks into his office. Miss Corsa is waiting for him.

Miss Corsa: Mr. Bowman said you might be interested in a two foot model of the MM Lancaster, and to quote him, 'Beauty bred to service.' I left it in my office.

Thatcher: Thank you for not bringing it in here, Miss Corsa. Send that mess back to Research, Miss Corsa, and tell Bowman that I am convinced there is no future in cars without running boards. It is bad enough Bowman has somehow persuaded the Committee to take a look at Michigan Motors but this too?

Miss Corsa: Yes, Mr. Thatcher. He's on his way to Detroit now.

Thatcher: Better him than me since this is his little adventure. I never did find out how he tricked the Investment Committee into sending him.

    A few minutes later. Miss Corsa steps in.

Miss Corsa: Mr. Thatcher, while leaving for Detroit, Mr. Bowman evidently broke his left ankle leaving a taxi at LaGuardia.

Thatcher: Miss Corsa, for a man who has been littering my desk with car information, I regard that as inexcusably clumsy. With Bowman in traction who goes off on this wild goose chase?

    Miss Corsa grimaces and then intercedes.

Miss Corsa: I'll send flowers and do you want to talk to Mr. Gabler?

Thatcher out loud: Everett is tied up negotiating credits; Charlie is reorganizing the liaison between the Trust and Collateral Departments, a move necessitated by the discovery that the innocents in Collateral Loans were lending money on securities the Trust Department had long since decided were worthless. Sinclair is in DC testifying; Blazdell is in Iraq and Innes has the mumps.

    Thatcher pauses and looks at Miss Corsa.

Mumps. What about Nicolls?

Miss Corsa: Too junior.

    Thatcher grasps for straws under Miss Corsa's lifted eyebrow.

Thatcher: Nonsense. It will do him good.

    Miss Corsa keeps her gaze.

Miss Corsa: Shall I book your flight for tomorrow morning?

Scene 8 -Int.-Krebbel's Office-Day

Thatcher enters Krebbel's office.

Thatcher: Good to see you Arnie.

Berman: Good morning, John. Let me introduce Glen Madsen, (40, tall, rugged, forbidding), MM's Planning and Research Director. And Miss Price (28, attractive, competent) who has some data for us.

She smiles and nods at Thatcher; Riley (30, handsome, aggressive) walks in looking for Miss Price.

Miss Price: You're not seeing these reports until I've typed them and sent them to Mr. Wahl or Mr. Jensen.

Riley: Listen Miss Price I know you were Jensen's secretary and now you're Wahl's so you're willing to fight all the way for Plantagenet. But I know as well as you do that Jensen has been keeping out of sight since he got back Monday. Either you give me that report or we check with Wahl...or...Madsen here.

Madsen: Excuse me gentlemen. What's the trouble, Riley?

Riley: Miss Price doesn't seem to know that our court order covers current records at Plantagenet, and she came in here for protection.

Berman: Court order?

Madsen: All right. Just give Riley any records he wants.

Price: Don't you think I should get Mr. Jensen to OK them first, Mr. Madsen?

Madsen: Give him the records.

Price: All right. Read it. But read it now. Mr. Wahl has to have it this afternoon..

Riley: Oh, the Tuesday Work Report. Let's see. Two cutters dismissed for brawling in the fender assembly men's room. Check with Thad and Grievance Committee. Guard Stanislaus Novotny's gun stolen...gun stolen! Why are people stealing guns at Plantagenet, Miss Price?

Price: To shoot snoopers.

Riley: Reported this to the police?

Price: Of course.

>Riley and Price leave.

Berman: What's this court order, Glen?

Madsen: Riley's from the DOJ. He's ensuring that MM complies with the cease and desist order.

>He pauses; with no comment he continues.

It's a darn nuisance you know. Only a formality. Around here price fixing is over for good.

>Krebbel walks in.

Krebbel: Good morning, gentlemen: Price fixing was a big problem. But I can assure you we've solved it. Glen, what about calling Ed Wahl. They can go through Plantagenet right after lunch.

>Madsen nodded his agreement.

We've got a Super Plantagenet we are building to the exact expectations of a Saudi Sheik. Ed Wahl's the man directing Plantagenet. Sorry I can't join you for lunch.

> Krebbel leaves. Arnie and Thatcher share a look.

Madsen: To save time we are having lunch here.

> Two men walk in laughing. Trays of sandwiches are brought in for them to choose lunch.

Madsen: Our Director and Assistant Director Research.

> Berman cuts in to break the ice and gets somewhere.

Berman: You boys look like you are having a good time.

Director of Research (Greyish 40 year old man): Buck's back. A great storyteller. You missed him. Managed to tell a great story combining disc brakes and bawdy tales. Nice to see that jail did not hamper his spirits. Buck says he met some great guys in jail.

> Madsen gives in as the director went on. Thatcher interjects.

Thatcher: What does Ray Jensen say about jail?

> This stops the conversation dead.

Madsen: Now we are going over to look at Plantagenet.

Thatcher: That is where they steal guns.

Berman: I don't blame them.

> Madsen notes the mood change.
>
> Pause.

Madsen: On second thought, why don't we stay here. You have seen lots of plants.

   Thatcher and Berman brighten up.

Berman: Now you are talking, Madsen. Break out the Scotch for John and me.

   Wahl walks in and a grin comes to his face.

Wahl: See you boys are starting to enjoy yourselves.

   They nod brightly. Wahl buzzes the secretary.

Wahl: Mabel, will you look for Mr. Jensen; tell him we are all here.

Madsen: When do we ship her, Ed?

Wahl: Tomorrow morning we are trucking her to New York. The Arabs arranged ocean freight. I hope they know how to tie her down securely.

Madsen: We are having a little cocktail party here so you won't have to go far. You'll want to meet our people. Too bad Jensen hasn't turned up; I asked Orin to tell him you'd be here.

Thatcher: Krebbel does a lot of leaving.

   They sit down and talk a bit. A few people arrive; they sit near each other and the waiter gets them drinks. One woman attaches herself to John after he escaped from two MM zealots.

Woman (Waspish 40, bedraggled, rich clothes): You are that big banker from New York?

   She says while hooking a large martini from a passing waiter.

Thatcher: Yes.

He misses her next words which are slurred from drink.

Thatcher: I beg your pardon?

Woman: I said things are awful at MM. It's that louse Jensen. It would be just like them to give him back his job. Why doesn't he just drop dead?

Diane Holzinger: Audrey! I am Diane Holzinger, Mr. Thatcher. Have you been introduced to Mrs. Wahl?

Thatcher starts to speak but Mrs. Wahl cuts him off.

Mrs. Wahl: Well, Di, how does it feel to have your husband out of jail?

By not so much as a flicker of an eyelash Di says with nothing more than indulgent tolerance for the rather drunk Mrs. Wahl.

Mrs. Holzinger: It's wonderful to have him home again. Being married to a business executive is an adventurous career, Mr. Thatcher. You have to be ready for anything.

John finds the lady's self-control formidable and impressive.

Mrs. Wahl: Ed didn't go to jail so don't give me that nonsense about all executives. And don't give me that superior look either, Di.

Mrs. Holzinger: I wonder if Ed is around anywhere.

Since a young man immediately detached himself from a nearby group to join theirs to moderate things, John rightfully concluded that Mrs. Wahl was a familiar problem at MM.

Mrs. Wahl continues.

Mrs. Wahl: Not that poor old Buck is to blame. He doesn't have enough brains, Ed says. It's that bum Jensen. You notice he isn't here, Di? For that matter I wonder where is Celia. Of course I can guess how she and Glen must be feeling. I don't know what they'd do about her divorce now.

    Di sharply.

Mrs. Holzinger: Audrey!

    Ed Wahl smoothly separatsd Audrey out.

Wahl: Audrey.

    John expells a sigh as he puts down his glass and prepares to move on. Di has other plans.

Mrs. Holzinger: A problem.

Thatcher: I'm sure it is. I think I see…

    He was outmatched by the smooth Mrs. Holzinger.

Mrs. Holzinger: Of course I'm sorry for Audrey, but you can see she's under strain. And of course there is always a reason for drinking.

    She smiles and leaves him alone for a moment.

Thatcher outloud: Indeed so and I have a reason for a drink in my own hotel room. Walter will not like my report; at least Ev, Charlie, and, yes, poor Nicolls, escaped this fiasco, and this is only the first day!

Scene 9 -Int.-Detroit Savings and Trust Conference Room- Day

    Thatcher walks in with a smile on his face.

Bank President (60ish well dressed banker type): I see John you are relieved to be here not there. This should make you happy to help us resolve the open credits between the Sloan and us as your correspondent bank locally.

Thatcher: Yes. And your generosity to let me have lunch here and not be taken somewhere in one of those cars, is a pleasure. Even Mack my driver couldn't help himself carrying on. I'll try to be more gracious to him on the way back.

Bank President: Don't worry John; Mack is used to it. Everyone at MM is. Heads will roll but they always do in the car business.

Thatcher would remember that line.

Scene 10-Int.-MM Lobby-Day

Thatcher walks into the lobby and is accosted.

Lincoln Hauser (40, thin, humorless): John Thatcher, well isn't this great. I've been hoping we'd run into each other. I heard you were here and I wanted to catch up with you to talk about old times. These Detroit people set a hard pace, a big change from the Sloan. MM frankly gives me more scope.

Lincoln Hauser, former Sloan PR director, was now the MM PR director as it turned out. Thatcher shows he is happy to be rid of him.

My first big job was to handle the price fixing scandal. A big challenge we handled well, if I do say. Here you grab the ball and carry it down the field--

Thatcher interrupts playfully.

Thatcher: I didn't know you were an athlete?

Hauser plows on; Thatcher girds himself for more.

Hauser: Tomorrow the Sheik himself will arrive for a presentation worth millions in free PR. It's been good to see you, Thatcher, and talk about the quiet old days at the Sloan. But I have to be ready when the Super Plantagenet arrives. Ah, there it is. I'll have to hurry off.

  Berman grimaces and comes over, with a number of aggressive MM juniors in pursuit.

Berman: John. Wait so I can join you.

  John waited. Berman finally comes over; Berman says lugubriously.

I can only take so much more of this. Even the driver of that car feels the same way; he drove in; alighted in his overalls, abandoned the car, and left going in the opposite direction from Hauser and crew. Smart man.

Thatcher: Do you remember Hauser?

Berman: Fortunately for you, John, no longer working at the Sloan.

  Thatcher nods and grins.

Better than with you John, and yes I do. Awful. They deserve each other.

  Both of them shrugged like dogs, smiled, and recovered their calm. Berman glides back into despair.

Thatcher: A full morning?

Berman: John, don't grin like that. At least you aren't in my situation, in the center, and you got out for the morning. Madsen marooned me with that bunch you saw with the charts. They even brought them to lunch and wouldn't stop.

Thatcher: Well then, the worst is over for you as the day is almost over. My sufferings are still before me. Which reminds me, hadn't we better get up to the Board Meeting in Krebbel's office?

Berman: No. Madsen said he would pick us up here in ten minutes.

Arnie sat comfortably and unwrapped a cigar. John recognized the symptoms. A fatalistic melancholia had settled over his companion in which escape from MM seemed impossible unless exit routes were close at hand. John sat down in a consoling gesture.

Krebbel emerged from the interior of the building, paused at the reception desk, and found his two guests sitting side by side pensively. Krebbel merely gave instructions to the receptionist about his upcoming chauffeured trip.

Krebbel: Tell them to give me a 2nd shift driver since he will have to take me home after the dinner. Also, I'll need that car to bring me back here tomorrow morning.

He addresses himself to them now.

Krebbel: I'll see you again tonight at the Chamber of Commerce Dinner.

A woman glides by. Berman cheers up instantly. Krebbel steps aside for her, says a word, and she comes over to Berman.

Berman: John, you haven't met Celia Jensen (40, attractive, a sparkle in her eye): Celia went to Cornell with my wife. Different sororities of course.

She laughs affectionately.

Mrs. Jensen: Arnie, you're still impossible but such a relief to have you here. I only wish Esther could have come too. You don't know what it has been like, and, anyway, I haven't seen her in ages with you being in New York and us out here.

Thatcher had never seen Arnie so energized and playful. John enjoys it.

Berman: You ought to come back with me. Esther would be surprised and tickled pink!

Her lips quivered slightly.

Mrs. Jensen: Oh, Arnie, you know I'd love to, but can't now.

Wistfully but forlornly.

Maybe later in the summer.

To John the conversation was becoming undesirably emotional. Apparently Celia agreed with him becauseshe almost immediately casts about for a calming topic.

Mrs. Jensen: Oh, I see they got the car here after all.

Berman: What car, Cele?

Mrs. Jensen: The Super Planty. Everyone at Plantagenet is behaving like a madman.

Berman: Oh. Been over there?

Mrs. Jensen: Yes. I've been looking for Ray. I haven't had a chance to talk to him since he got back last Monday and this situation is maddening for all of us. We closed down the house before the trial and I stayed with my sister. When I saw Krebbel's Drake pulling into the parking lot I thought I had finally caught up to Ray. But up in Ray's office Wahl said no. Evidently Frank has been looking for him too. And Frank just told me Ray isn't here now either. Nobody seems to know where he is.

Berman: Playing hard to get.

The interruption recalled Celia to her anecdote.

Mrs. Jensen: While Ed and I were talking the door flew open and one of the engineers roared that the Super Planty was being stolen.

Arnie returns to his regular sobersides posture.

Berman: $150,000 worth of car!

She laughs.

Mrs. Jensen: I thought Ed was going to explode. Then we all went racing down to the garage to see the tail lights disappearing out the door.

Arnie interjects,

Berman: I've always had my doubts about MM management.

Celia continues.

Mrs. Jensen: Ed went wild. No one could stop him as he went pounding after it, shaking his fist. I was the only one who could laugh because everyone else worked for Ed.

Thatcher: Hauser and his people undoubtedly have that effect. At the Sloan we didn't give him quite the same scope but I always thought he would make a first rate horse thief.

Arnie stayed Arnie through this mild amusing remark and continued being critical about executives chasing after cars shouting and waving their fists.

Berman: John we better get upstairs for the Board meeting since Madsen is late.

They made their farewells to Celia with Arnie adding a fraternal kiss, and then proceeded toward the elevator.

Just as Celia crossed the lobby, Madsen appeared.

Winters: Mr. Madsen, have you seen the driver?

Madsen: What driver?

Winters: The one who drove the Super Planty here. I was in the car with him but he's taken off. We want to photo someone in overalls near the car.

Madsen: Haven't seen him, why don't you just put on some overalls yourself? Or go around the building.

Winters darts off in pursuit.

Berman: Glen, where is Ray?

Madsen: Don't know.

Scene 11-Int.-Krebbel's Office-Day

Thatcher and Berman walk in. With no sense of irony French speaks.

French: I can see we're all looking forward to this meeting.

Berman: Now, about your depreciation system.

The meeting continues.

Madsen: We thought we could speed things along if we skipped the planned drinks at the Wahls and just have drinks and dinner here.

The sighs of relief are heard from Berman and Thatcher.

Buck: Ed, have you found Ray?

Wahl: No I haven't been able to track Ray down, Ed, but I can tell you one thing--

as Buck cut him off.

Buck: Never mind, never mind. Ray will turn up tomorrow when all the Super Planty pictures are taken, guess who will turn up trying to hog all the PR, throw his weight around, and try to grab all the credit, Ed? Ray Jensen, that's who.

Madsen: Shut up Buck.

Buck: Yes, our friend Ray. The man who always stands up for his friends. The man who covers up for them when they're in trouble, the man who came right back to MM to take over!

At the another table Krebbel was coming ponderously to a conclusion.

Krebbel: On the basis of past performance, we see room for nothing but confidence in MM's future.

Thatcher and Berman share a look.

Scene 12-Int.-Krebbel's Office Next Day-Day

Berman and Thatcher walk in. No one there.

Thatcher: Arnie, we are going to finish today, one way or the other, and escape to New York.

Arnie grimaces and nods. Buck walks in.

Buck: The big ceremony is going on downstairs, but I take it you want to just get this done and escape. Can't say I blame you. The big unanswered question is whether Ed or Ray represents the company. Not your cup of tea.

Buck grins.

Berman: Quite right. We will stay up here out of it, blessedly. Please let Krebbel and Madsen know to send up whoever they want us to talk with. We are leaving at 12 noon for the airport.

Buck grins again, nods, and leaves. Thatcher and Arnie attend to their paperwork. Mrs. Jensen walks in.

Mrs. Jensen: Was told you were here. I'm so ashamed. I don't know what to say.

Berman: Now, Cele, don't worry about that. Just take it easy and you don't have to say anything if you don't want to.

Mrs. Jensen: But I've got to tell you. Ray's just lost control. I can't believe the things he's saying. I wasn't looking for him you know. I just bumped into him. And he said you just have to decide what it is you want and then go out and get it. But it's the way he looked while he said it. I tell you, Arnie, I am frightened. I never thought things would come to this.

Berman: When did you meet him?

Mrs. Jensen: 30 minutes ago. On the other side of the building. It's deserted with everyone over here.

Berman: What set him off? Or was it just seeing you?

Mrs. Jensen: No, that is, let's not talk about it anymore, Arnie. And Mr. Thatcher, oh dear, I know I've behaved like a fool and I'm so sorry to have inflicted this upon you. Mr. Krebbel has sidelined everyone but himself to make the presentation downstairs.

Madsen walks in grimly.

Madsen: First that Hauser started firing at the Planty to show it could survive such an semi automatic attack then he swung open the rear door and found a bloodied head and shoulders of Ray Jensen. Then the screaming started with Audrey Wahl being the worst.

He hugs Celia.

I am sorry it had to end this way for you Celia.

Krebbel and several police walk in.

Krebbel: Gentlemen, Ray is dead as it would seem Madsen has told you. The police thought this would be a good place to review the situation and interview the witnesses.

Thatcher, Berman, Mrs. Jensen, and Madsen leave.

Scene 13-Int.-Telegraph Motel & Fuel House Bar-Night

Thatcher and Berman are in the Fuel House bar.

Berman: This is going to be a mess. That Hauser of yours....

Thatcher cuts in.

Thatcher: Not mine anymore, thank goodness. A bad omen when I saw him. So we are told he fires a semi-automatic at the car, scares everyone, looks like he killed Jensen, then faints as if having a heart attack, making the situation even worse. So he can't even capitalize on the most newsworthy event of his life.

Berman: And then we have the news hawks even selling them in the dining room, screaming headlines, Vehicle of Death, and so on.

Shakes his head mournfully with Thatcher.

It could be worse, I guess, but I am not sure how. Any facts?

Saginaw parts dealer down the bar: Won't be until the later editions. The newsboys will bring them in here. Good day for them.

They did.

Berman: Hugh thinks I should stick around this weekend. Thank goodness Madsen was there for Celia. Esther says that at least Celia won't have to go through the divorce. Practical that woman just like your Miss Corsa.

Arnie is getting in a better mood as he helps himself to salted peanuts and tosses off his drink. He continues in a slightly disrespectful tone about his boss.

Hugh says that maybe we will have to defer this stock issue until the mess here is cleared up. No kidding.

They shake their heads in unison.

Thatcher: Yes. That's the line Bowman has sold our Investment Committee. Don't worry. With the market behaving the way it has been, and recent events here, MM won't be issuing any stock for a long while.

A newsboy comes in and starts doing business.

Ah there are the evening papers.

Their second drinks arrive at the same time.

Berman: Can't help themselves talking about cars. Even with this they start by paying homage to the Super Planty before getting down to it. Makes me glad I am a subway rider.

Thatcher reads.

"State Police Captain Georgeson announced that the preliminary lab reports indicate the dead man was slain sometime Wednesday. There was no connection with the gunfire today. Jensen's body was placed on the car's rear seat floor after death. Experts as yet can't determine whether the victim was shot in the car or not. The car was on public display and unguarded for 24 hours. It was in an area restricted to MM employees and their guests. The Super Planty itself has been impounded by the State Police for further investigation."

Berman: Mm. That puts the finger on someone in the inner circle, doesn't it? The car was unguarded for 24 hours, in an area virtually restricted to our friends, the MM executives.

Thatcher: And their guests and families.

>Arnie frowns but does not rise to the bait directly.

Berman: Assume that Ray's body could have been dumped in the car only when there wasn't a crowd around it. Then it was only last night or early this morning it was done. Remember Buck said people started showing up far earlier than usual today.

Thatcher: Of course Jensen's body could have been in the Plantagenet all the time.

Berman: It is possible. But obviously the police are going to start digging around for motives.

>Thatcher finishes the thought.

Thatcher: ...of which there are many.

>Arnie brightens somewhat.

Berman: Yes. Plenty of people wanted Ray out of the way.

>And he is interrupted by a neighbor.

Neighbor: You have said a mouthful. I am in the car business too. Rentals.

Berman nods to the neighbor and speaks to Thatcher.

Berman: Have you seen this? An inside memo urging all members of the MM family to refrain from discussing the murder. Also an HR executive rebuking the security staff for laxity in preventing the theft of firearms.

And, John, the memo continues: The police have informed us that the murder weapon was a service revolver of the same make and caliber as those issued to MM guards. Such a revolver had been stolen from guard headquarters at the Plantagenet building just last Tuesday.

Thatcher: I look forward to MM's take on it. Ready to have dinner Arnie? I have to call Brad first.

Thatcher calls from a phone at the bar. Arnie leaves.

Brad Withers V.O.: Sorry to kill your escape plan, John., but I was talking to George.

Thatcher grimaces.

Thatcher: OK Brad, I'll stay.

Hangs up.

Of course Miss Corsa would know that my curiosity would probably get the better of me so I won't call her or she'll hear it in my voice. Brad can think I am martyred. Good.

Berman returns to the bar restaurant to see John pushing away a pile of papers.

Berman: Hugh may have to invest in drying me out after all this. French is pretending everyone loved Jensen and everything is just hunky dory.

Thatcher: Well, what else can he say?

Arnie almosts barks.

Berman: He could keep quiet, couldn't he?

Thatcher: There is that Arnie. Yes, that would be the best course. But without silence we're left without much to say for the facts have to be faced. The gun was stolen there on Tuesday, the day before Jensen's murder. Makes it look premeditated.

Berman: I know, I know. And they have to explain how Jensen could be missing from Wednesday to Friday without anyone reporting it. They can't very well issue a PR release saying Jensen was such an SOB people were glad he was lying low. Or that he was such an annoyance they were grateful he wasn't around. But still, I wish French would shut up.

Thatcher nods as he is expected to do.

Thatcher: And Mrs. Jensen?

Berman: She's going to be in real trouble thanks to Audrey. You remember that business she blurted out to us and evidently did before downstairs before the presentation..

Thatcher: I've been remembering it vividly for the last two days.

Berman: That Wahl woman heard it and gave the police a hyped up version that put Celia into the soup. She said Celia was talking about running into Ray. And Celia, the little idiot, went along with that story. That was Friday afternoon, when the police finally talked to her. Then when they realized how long he had been dead, they got after her. And she gave some story about quarreling with some maintenance person about where she parked her car. You can see how all that would look to the police.

Thatcher lifts an eyebrow.

Thatcher: I'm not sure they don't look that way to me.

    Gloom settled over Arnie. He seems comfortable in gloom like Gabler.

Berman: Me too. But whatever she has been up to, she doesn't deserve more trouble. Frankly she is at the breaking point. The last year clearly hasn't been easy for her. Now this. And the police will be on her until she tells them the truth about Friday morning.

Berman: What I need is another drink.

    Monday morning.

Read this little charmer of a newsletter to start off our week.

    Thatcher reads it out loud.

"Well, one of our stocks that got rained on last week, Michigan Motors, known as MM, and I don't think it will dry out soon. In fact I am feeling bearish about all auto stocks now. Of course people will keep buying cars. But they do so emotionally not reasonably. And who wants money tied up in an industry where their executives are either in jail or shot up? Jensen dropped from sight for a few days and no one says they saw him. Odd, to say the least. Now if you are looking for a speculative stock, look on the OTC market. High voltage generators may be the coming thing."

    Monday night at the bar.

Berman: Even Hugh is tired of this. Ordered me back. Keep on eye on Celia for me, will you John.

    Thatcher nods.

I wish Hugh would make up his mind whether he's hot or cold on MM. And I wish I knew why you are staying John. Don't tell me it's because Walter had sold the Investment Committee. The MM issue is a dead duck as you have said before.

    Thatcher tries to sound dignified.

Thatcher: I'm curious. If American industry has just developed a new method for solving executive personnel problems, I believe it is my responsibility to keep the Sloan informed.

    Berman looks at Thatcher sideways but keeps his lips buttoned.

Scene 14-Int.-Lansing Rectory-Day

    John is sitting in the living room.

Mrs. Prescott (60, round): So you are a friend of Mrs. Jensen's. I am afraid she is low, very low indeed. The Reverend and her sister have tried to bring her along.

Thatcher: In the Episcopal faith you mean?

Prescott (60, robust): Of course.

    Thatcher has an involuntary glance of appeal to Celia's sister but this only leads to his hostess producing a platter of tastefully arranged finger sandwiches.

Thatcher: I see.

Prescott: This function represents the terminal activity of the monthly meeting of the St. Andrew's Altar Guild. A very important meeting.

    John is heard to groan slightly. Thatcher shifts his legs slightly, being crushed between 2 matrons.

Thatcher: I beg your pardon, Miss Tickbourne.

Miss Tickbourne (60, thin): Mr. Thatcher, would a cope make the more appropriate gift for the rector? Hand embroidered of course.

Thatcher: Naturally, as you say.

Prescott: I understood that the Committee had agreed on the cope.

Tickbourne: But a Eucharistic vestment, somehow it shows so much more feeling, and dear Father Burns is so sensitive to these distinctions.

Prescott: That sort of talk may be very well under certain circumstances Lavinia but it is an awkward way to refer to a married man. Almost indelicate.

With battlelines drawn, Thatcher found himself between them on the couch. Tickborne brings out a letter and several ladies shudder as they leap into speech.

Mrs. Fulham (50ish, round): We all know that Mr. Burns is sensitive. Mrs. Jensen being his sister-in-law makes things so difficult for him just now. Bad enough when she was living apart from her husband. But now. All this notoriety. Naturally the rector is upset.

John glanced across the room where Burns was happily the center of attention.

Tickbourne looks torn between the gossip and the letter; puts the letter away to the obvious relief of the other ladies.

Tickbourne: I understand that Mrs. Jensen point-blank refused to rejoin her husband. And only a few days before his...er...death.

Mrs. Fulham: But there was a reconciliation.

Prescott: Just a sham. It was only for the look of things during his trial.

    Thatcher sniffs the scent and speaks.

Thatcher: I had not realized the disagreement was of such long standing.

Prescott: One might almost say that the disagreements date from their marriage.

Fulham: Jensen was not what one would hope for in a husband. Totally wrapped up in his work, not much interested in a family life, and there were no children.

    The 3 ladies sigh. Tickbourne is aroused.

Tickbourne: That is no excuse for a wife to leave her husband. Whatever his faults, there was no talk of separation until last summer. Not until when Mrs. Jensen met Mr. Madsen.

Prescott: Now there, I think we have a great deal of smoke and very little fire..

Fulham: No. Edgar played golf with Belton the other day. He said Jensen went to Ann Arbor to have it out with Madsen. They had a terrible quarrel by all reports. The neighbors almost called the police. The whole university is talking about it. So there must be something to it.

Thatcher: When was this?

Fulham: Sometime last week. Just after Mrs. Jensen said she wouldn't be leaving Lansing.

    An ornately dressed woman enters.

Tickbourne: Mary Ellen has to get back to her children. She comes to play the organ at our service; always so faithful.

The ladies shuffle out on cue, leaving Burns and Thatcher alone.

Rector Burns (40, priggish) Glad you enjoyed it. Let's see. You wanted to speak to Celia. She should be back shortly.

Mrs. Burns walks in to clear the table.

Mrs. Burns: Was Mary Ellen after you for confession again?

Rector Burns: Well, as a matter of fact, yes. She wants to come in tomorrow before school lets out.

Mrs. Burns: I really don't see why she can't make do with the General Confession like everyone else.

Rector Burns: Confession is an established prerogative of the Anglican believer. When the need is felt--

Mrs. Burns cuts him off, as if it is a familiar refrain.

Mrs. Burns: Yes, yes. What's more considering she is raising three children, without help, taking care of a large Victorian house, and spending every free minute at St. Andrew's, it doesn't seem as if she'd have much material for you.

Rector Burns: There are sins of the mind, Louise.

Mrs. Burns: If we could just settle the ones of the body first, I'd be happier.

Celia makes a well timed entry to end the conversation. She sinks down on the sofa next to John.

All of this slinking around doesn't do any good. You should have stayed for the Guild and seen some new faces.

Celia chuckles.

Mrs. Jensen: And deprive everyone of the chance to gossip?

Rector Burns: Nobody gossiped.

    The two sisters look at him impatiently,

Mrs. Burns: Oh, Larry, not in front of you.

Mrs. Jensen: Did anyone talk about anything else?

    John answers trying to shift the subject.

Thatcher: Yes. Miss Tickbourne wanted to talk about someone named Father John.

Mrs. Burns: Lavinia has been writing to the Crowley Fathers again.

Mrs. Jensen: Is she going to publish?

Rector Burns: For heaven's sake, Celia, why in the world would she do so?

Mrs. Jensen: Well everyone seems to.

    The Rector abandons the field in the face of superior forces.

Rector Burns: In any event, Mr. Thatcher has not been waiting to hear us discuss this.

    For the first time Celia seems to realize Thatcher's presence must be on her account.

Mrs. Jensen: Oh, that is thoughtful of him. And you too, of course. But what can anyone do to help?

The Burns hastily started to leave. She impatiently waved them back to their seats.

Do you think I'm going to reveal my secrets. There aren't any. There isn't even anything to talk about. All I can do is grin and bear it.

John tut-tutted sympathetically and the rector made an ill-advised remark about Madsen.

It isn't his fault. He's suffering as much as I am.

Pompously the Rector speaks.

Rector Burns: Nevertheless you would never be in this position if you hadn't left your husband. Today everyone seems to think that marriage can be turned on and off like an electric light.

Celia cuts in.

Mrs. Jensen: We are talking about murder here, not divorce.

Thatcher: Precisely. And, it must be talked about, putting it bluntly. You aren't doing Madsen or yourself any good by lying to the police. After all, the presentation was 2 days after the murder. You're not achieving anything other than creating an air of collusion.

Mrs. Jensen: I'm not lying to the police anymore. I told the Captain that it was Glen I was talking to Friday at MM. I had to. Someone saw us. And I've explained to him we were quarreling. That's why I was upset. It wasn't about anything important.

Thatcher: You told Arnie and me Ray not Glen was out of control, that you were frightened about what he might do. There must have been a more significant reason.

Her stubborn silence was eloquent. Thatcher played a hunch,

Thatcher: Was it about the Ann Arbor quarrel?

Mrs. Jensen: You know about that?

Thatcher: It is common gossip. I heard it in this very room. If the police don't know yet, they soon will.

Mrs. Jensen: But you don't understand. It was Ray who was furious not Glen. Glen just laughed it off when Ray started to threaten.

Thatcher: Threaten?

Mrs. Jensen: Yes. It all started when Ray came to see me here. I suppose the Altar Guild brought you up to date on that too.

    John nods.

Ray said he wasn't going to sit still for a divorce. But I'd been to a divorce lawyer and said I would go to Nevada if need be. That frightened him. Because in spite of his toughness that was where he was most vulnerable. MM doesn't approve of divorce. With his job in the air, this could have been the final factor. Ray was angry he had to deal with me when he needed to be full time at MM to reassert his position. And, of course, he ran the marriage up until this first time when he didn't have his way. When he left here he must have decided to put pressure on Glen to stop the divorce.

Mrs. Burns: How could he? Glen was the one urging divorce.

Mrs. Jensen: That's because you never understood how Ray's mind worked. He went straight for what he thought was Glen's jugular. Ray said if I went to Nevada he would see to it Glen lost his job. Ray would let the front office know Glen seduced me and he'd get fired.

Thatcher: And would they have?

Mrs. Jensen: But Glen didn't seduce me.

Mrs. Burns speaks quickly to head off her husband.

Mrs. Burns: Larry, this is no time for a lot of talk about sins of the mind.

Mrs. Jensen: Glen didn't really care about his job. He told Ray to do his worst. We were going through with the divorce. That's what infuriated Ray. He never contemplated such a reaction. As far as he was concerned everyone lived and died for MM.

Thatcher: But if Madsen was so unmoved by the threat why was he in such a murderous rage just two days later?

Mrs. Jensen: Gossip started to work. Some was getting back to Ray. Orin Dunn relayed to him some of the spicier parts. I think Orin wanted some kind of deal; he would help Ray if Ray helped him.

Just then the doorbell rang. Mrs. Burns goes out to answer it.

Thatcher: There's one thing, if Ray started this gossip as a result of his rebuff, it may be possible to prove Dunn saw your husband alive after his return from Ann Arbor Tuesday evening.

The horror of that statement drained blood from her face.

Mrs. Jensen: You mean the police may think that Ray died *that* night?

Thatcher: If the time is medically possible, yes.

Mrs. Jensen: Oh, no. That couldn't be possible.

Mrs. Burns comes back in.

Mrs. Burns: Mr. Riley is here from the DOJ. He wants to talk to you, Celia. It would be a good idea. Antagonizing him won't help you.

Mrs. Jensen: I won't. He wants to ask me about Ray's business dealings. Ray never told me anything about them and now I don't care about that at all. I don't care about anything but Glen. He didn't kill Ray; even if he did, I would still love him.

  John saw that all the cards, or at least most of them, seemed to be on the table. He sat back to let things further unfold.

Don't start, Louise. Oh don't you see? I wasted 10 years of my life with Ray. I can't give up whatever happiness I have a chance for now. I won't. I won't.

  The Rector, a man inured to feminine crises, moves agilely towards the door with the word, "tea," and made his escape as Louise and Celia do too. John leaves the room and brings Riley back in.

Riley: I suppose she isn't going to see me.

Thatcher: No. She's too focused on her husband's death to have the energy for his business difficulties.

Riley: She sounds upset. I'm sorry. But the two may be connected, you know.

Thatcher: Yes. I'm interested in Jensen's murder and MM. Sometime we might discuss the matter.

Riley: Yes. I'd like to do that sometime. We might come up with something useful. I have to check some other things out first.

  Riley leaves and Thatcher does soon thereafter.

Thatcher out loud to himself: Jensen said people lived and died for MM. Perhaps he did just that.

Scene 15-Int.-Laundromat-Day

Riley is in the laundromat waiting for one of the devices to empty. Suddenly his chart disappears under a falling drift of white material. Somebody was scattering laundry over him. He grabbed the cloth and prepared to deal more effectively with the toddler. But there was no child in sight, only the back of a woman emptying the nearby dryer.

Riley: Ahem.

Miss Price: What? Oh did I overshoot the basket. I'm so...why, Mr. Riley!

Riley: Miss Price. At first I didn't recognize you. Here. I guess this is yours.

Susan Price blushes. Gravely Riley examines the object he was extending her which was as chaste a slip as one could imagine, except possibly for the embroidered forget-me-knots on the lacy hem, rather favorably comparing with most of the lingerie that had come his bachelor's way.

Miss Price: Thank you.

Riley: It's quite a respectable slip.

Susan grins appreciatively.

Price: I know it seems silly. After all, every week I scatter my underwear around in front of strangers. But I don't expect to meet people I know. What are you doing here?

Riley: My laundry. They said it would be 3 days at the hotel, and far more expensive, so I didn't want to wait and it is cheaper.

Price: Yes. And I see you are not wasting time. Doing your homework for tomorrow's snooping?

    Riley stiffens.

Riley: Well, you have to admit MM's given the DOJ plenty of grounds for snooping.

Price: Everything was fine until you and the others came sneaking around, stirring things up. Now it just gets worse and worse. We have you, the police, and the Captain himself. And everyone's beginning to look hunted and suspicious. Why can't you just leave us alone? Oh what's the use? I don't even understand what I'm talking about.

You wouldn't believe it, but the binding just melted and glazed.

Riley: I'm sorry. Look here, you can't pretend everyone at MM is a lily white innocent.

Price: Oh can't I? What about the poor PR guy riding along in the Plantagenet? They've been grilling him for days. He's only been here for two weeks. We never saw him in the front office; he was only following orders.

Blanket Dryer: Can I borrow that pen?

    Susan nods.

Riley: And the gun. I suppose that was another coincidence being stolen in the company plant.

Price: Oh, the gun. You can't imagine the trouble that's causing us. Mr. Casmir from the union is claiming that it's all a management plot to implicate a union man.

Blanket dryer: That's right. Those big shots will blame it all on the Working Man, you wait and see. Here's your pen. Thank you very much. What I wrote will make them sit up and take notice.

>The departure of this believer in class warfare left Susan to glare at Riley.

Price: See. That's the kind of feeling the union will cash in on. And on top of everything else, he's claiming the driver of the Planty wasn't one of his people, when everyone knows we are a union shop.

Riley: But what's that got--

>He hears himself and softens his tone.

But, you know, you can't pretend the trouble is that people are asking questions about the gun and the car. The trouble started because someone murdered Ray Jensen.

>Price notices the softened tone and responds in kind.

Price: I suppose you are right. But you can't imagine what things are like in the office. It is plain awful.

Riley: Captain Georgeson isn't hounding you or anything?

>A sudden quirk lifts the corner of her mouth.

Price: Oh, no. It isn't anything like that. In fact he's more polite to me than you are. I suppose I'm looking back to the good old days when I worked for Mr. Jensen. At least you knew where you were.

Riley: You know, you've always been loyal about his activities but I can't help noticing that you don't seem to be very much grieved by his death.

Price: Yes, that's true. But it was terribly hard to feel close to him, you know, even though I worked for him for almost 2 years. He was completely dehumanized. Everything was routine and procedure. Of course that did make working for him easy. And then there was never any doubt about his authority, so there weren't any of those squabbles defending his interests. But I couldn't mourn him like a friend. He had been gone six months; that's a long time at Michigan Motors.

Riley: Here, let me get that. Wahl must be a very different type to work with.

Price: He is much nicer. Grumpier but human; of course he's more nervous, but that's only natural. He was over in Trucks for years. And he isn't a front office type. Then it didn't help any to get an acting appointment. And having people come back and start thumbing through his files was just about the last--

Riley: So Jensen was combing the division files. You know, I would have thought he knew everything there was to know about Plantagenet.

Price: It wasn't just Plantagenet. It was *all* the files.

Riley: He might have been trying to catch up on what happened while he was away. Of course you didn't notice the time period he was interested in.

Price: You're wrong on both counts.

Riley: So he was going back through last year. What a situation! He must have been dead serious about finding the tipster.

Price: He was serious about everything..

Riley: Yes, I can see how things were easier under Jensen. And of course he was primed to be your next president. So that added to his prestige.

Price: Well, certainly everyone expected him to become president. But you know, I'm not so sure he would have been as good a choice as Mr. Krebbel. For one thing, he was never interested in compacts. He'd been in Plantagenet so long he wasn't well-rounded. And then he could never handle people well. Mr. Krebbel is wonderful at that.

After the trial I didn't think anyone could organize the front office again. But he had everything running smoothly by the end of the year. Somehow he managed to make everyone feel optimistic, as if the worst was over and it was going to be better from then on. And this last month he's had to smooth down both Mr. Jensen and Mr. Wahl, and he's tried to keep Mr. Dunn from nosing around. He always tries to be tactful, which a lot of bosses don't worry about. And, he never blames the secretaries. He knows we can't do anything about it.

Riley: What was Dunn nosing around for? Did he want to see the same things Jensen was interested in?

Price: Well, naturally he was interested in who did the tipping too. He-- That's funny. I never thought about that before. It is so natural to think of him as Jensen's shadow. You know that's what they called him here. But he is not interested in the same files; he was always trying to get into this year's files.

It wasn't only Plantagenet either. I know Eileen was practically in tears when he sneaked Lancaster budget material off her desk during her lunch. She went to Krebbel about it. She was sure Dunn photocopied it. Krebbel was wonderful according to her. That's what I mean about him. Said it wasn't her fault and not to be upset. MM didn't expect her to have to guard against that sort of thing.

Riley: Sure, Krebbel's wonderful.

Price: He is. He treats us as if we are people; in the front office that is something.

Riley: It is easy for him to be agreeable now. He's on top.

Price: That shows how prejudiced you are. He's always been that way. Last year he was just controller and very nice to me. I rushed out to my car one night and threw packages into it. Then I went back for my gloves. When I got back I thought my car was gone. I had mixed up his Drake with mine. He didn't know what to do with 20 shamrock cupcakes I had for that night. But the next day he brought in a cake with an inscription, 'For the Day after St. Patrick's.' Wasn't that sweet?

Riley: Just grand.

 Susan sighed and looked around for inspiration.

Price: If those green and white shorts are yours you better empty the dryer. There done. Here, that's no way to do it. Everything will get wrinkled.

Riley: It is all very well for you to blow up every time someone speaks slightingly of your precious MM, but you have to admit that there are some very queer things going on there.

 She retorts.

Price: There are queer things going on in every company.

Riley: Not the kind of queerness that ends up with someone stealing a gun and shooting.

 She was swinging a sock lightheartedly and he grabbed it from her.

Will you be serious. This is no joking matter.

Price: Yes it is very serious. And I really don't know what is going on. Mr. Jensen was easy to figure out. But Mr. Wahl is not. And Mr. Dunn is creeping around. He was always a snoop but now there's an intensity about him that almost frightens me.

It is as if he himself were scared stiff of what he's doing, but determined to go through with it.

Harried mother: Excuse me. Would either of you have two nickels for a dime?

Price: I'll see. I'm afraid I can't find any. Oh, here's one.

    Finds a nickel and gives it to her.

Harried mother: Thank you so much. They only take nickels for the bleach.

    Her departure left them staring at each other with some constraint. To break it up Susan poked her head into the dryer to find a missing soc.k

Price: I knew it must be somewhere.

Riley: Now Susan, I'm sorry about--

Price: Mr. Riley, if you are going to call me Susan perhaps I had better know your first name.

    Silence.

Price: Well.

Riley: It is Fabian Xerxes. Father was a socialist.

    Susan was thoughtful for a moment as she patted the last of the pile into place. Then she giggled slightly. Fabian Xerxes raised an affronted eyebrow. She sobered.

Price: Fabian is a respectable name.

    And then he went blank before grinning. A dimple appeared on her face. He reached out a long arm and drew her laundry cart next to his own.

Riley: A drink? Dinner? Movie?

Price: I think there is something I should tell you first.

Riley: Yes?

Price: My name is Susan B. Anthony Price. Mother was a feminist.

Scene 16-Int.-Holzinger Party Living Room-Night

Thatcher outloud: Mrs. Holzinger has used her skill to gather the remaining *outs*, namely her husband and the Orin Dunns, and any *ins* who could be prevailed upon to receive them back into the MM fold. This house is more than paid for than by MM, a lot more.

Lionel French: Thatcher, glad you could make it. Di throws great parties; we are so glad she came here from Chicago.

>Thatcher lifts an eyebrow to pull a card.

Oh yes, she's one of the Chicago Bredons. Meat packing family, you know.

Thatcher: Indeed I do. They have a chapter to themselves in every standard history of the great America fortunes, and I as a banker commend that. So they are no way dependent on Michigan Motors, eh French?

French: Exactly so. Why they can show a little panache and independence others can't.

>They shared a look. Hauser intruded. Thatcher took note French left him stranded.

Hauser: But money isn't everything, Thatcher, not here at least. Out here it is achievement that counts. Not how much money you have.

Thatcher struggled to keep a straight face.

Hauser: Di is a simple toiler in the vineyard of industrial progress. You couldn't go further wrong than to think Di is just another parasite. Why you should have seen her when Buck came up with the Drake. She was starry-eyed. That's what she wants. A sense of accomplishment.

Thatcher couldn't help himself.

Thatcher: Offhand, you know, one would expect it to be her husband who had the sense of accomplishment.

Hauser: Ah, but Di was the woman behind the man behind the compact. Just think of it! She always makes it clear that at MM she's only operating as Buck's wife.

Di puts her hand on French's arm to attract his attention as Hauser continues.

Hauser: I was just letting Thatcher know how highly we all think of Di.

Buck smiles and led everyone into dinner. The dinner group is small so they all fall into one conversation.

French mutters: Shocking.

Buck: What's that?

Di: Lionel is disturbed about Gleason and Tom Halliday going to smaller auto companies.

Buck: There's nothing to get excited about. The boys have to take care of themselves. Nobody's got any right to say they shouldn't. Heck, we're all in the same spot.

Orin Dunn: Who says we're all in the same spot? That's not the way it looks from where I sit. Was Jensen in the same spot?

French: Now, now. De Mortuis and all that.

Dunn: De Mortuis, hell. Jensen steps off that train and he's in Krebbel's office for 2 hours. I want to talk to Frank too. Do I get in? We got here over a week ago and he still hasn't found time to see me.

Hauser: You're forgetting Ray's position aren't you? Orin old boy? After all he is senior management. It's only natural that Frank wanted to talk to him right away.

 Orin shrills.

Dunn: Senior management. He was so senior he was responsible for the whole price fixing mess. How do you think I got mixed up in it? He put the bite on me for sales. Then when the pressure was on he squealed like a pig. First he railroaded me into this fix, then he sent me up the river.

 French reproachfully.

French: Ray did not...er...squeal.

Dunn: The hell he didn't. If Jensen had his way, I would have taken the rap alone. My God, when the Feds first came around--

 Di cut in.

Di: Now Orin...

Dunn: Do you know what Jensen said to me last week? He said his future plans at Plantagenet didn't include me. He said my jail record would be a handicap.

Buck: Now that is just about the limit.

Dunn: Don't think I'm through yet. Oh sure it would be convenient for everyone if I shut up like a good boy. Do you expect me to forget that if it hadn't been for those photostats of the code I was going to get thrown to the wolves all by myself.

Do you expect me to take that lying down? Well, I didn't work for Jensen for 5 years without learning a thing or two. They've got some surprises coming to them.

French: We all know Frank is very fair. Like everyone else at Michigan Motors, he is fully aware of the contribution to the company's welfare made by the timely introduction of the compact. Furthermore, he is always interested in hearing the views of others, and of an opportunity to thrash out any differences of opinion which may exist. I have every confidence that any decision he may reach will reflect the best interests of the company and the public.

Dunn: That's fine. So he takes into account that the compact was a good thing--and maybe even the sales of the Plantagenet too--and then he decides it is in the best interests of the company to kick us out. I suppose that's expected to satisfy us.

Di: That won't happen. Not if it is handled properly. But you will have to pull yourself together Orin, if you want to make a good impression on Frank. I realize you are upset, but you mustn't let it affect your judgment.

 Mrs. Dunn enters the conversation.

Mrs. Dunn: Of course he is upset. Orin has been under a terrible strain. First there were weeks and weeks of pressure during the trial and being on public view. Then six months in jail with common criminals. Just imagine what an ordeal it must have been for someone like Orin. And then to come back to a murder. And all of this without a word of complaint. Naturally it's been almost more than he could bear. And darling, I think it's *good* for you to get some of this off your chest. It can't be healthy to repress your natural feelings. I'm sure you must feel better now that you've told us frankly what you think.

 Paralyzed silence. Then Buck as the host speaks.

Buck: Well, I don't deny you had a raw deal and I hope things work out.

Di: Yes, we all hope so.

> They step away from the table and 3 men have a brandy.

French: If you ask me, that young man is unbalanced.

> Hauser babbles something.

I have the greatest respect for Di Holzinger, but I am at a loss to understand what she sees in him. Not that I regret having prevailed upon Frank to see the boy. Everyone should have his day in court. That is to say it is only right he should be given an opportunity to explain things from his point of view.

Thatcher: I thought his complaint, or at least one of them, was that Krebbel hasn't seen him.

French: Not yet. But he is going to tomorrow morning. After all the boy's been haunting the executive offices for days now. It is time his status was...er...clarified.

> French poured himself more brandy.

I had hoped that Buck would come along. The cool detachment of an older head you know ... invaluable. These occasions can be pretty difficult. In fact, I don't see the point of the meeting without Buck. So why does Di insist on it?

Hauser: Perhaps she is interested in Dunn's future because they are all in the same boat.

French: Nonsense...she's always taken an interest in the careers of the young people in Michigan. Feels a sense of responsibility. But still, why does she bother with Dunn?

> The question about Di remained on the table when the evening ended.

Scene 17-Int.-Diner-Day

The next morning Krebbel and Thatcher were scheduled to have a meeting downtown with the financial staff.

Thatcher calls Krebbel at another office.

Thatcher V.O.: I have another meeting so won't be seeing you at your financial meeting.

Krebbel V.O.: I have another appointment too.

Thatcher walks into a promising looking diner, with no attraction for the expense account crowd. He gets the special and sits at a long table with one other occupant at Guido's Cafeteria.

Thatcher looks up and sees the healthy owner of his healthy meal. He found himself looking into a pleasantly neutral face, characterized by nothing more remarkable than a retreating hairline and rimless glasses. Looking in fact at the face of Frank Krebbel.

Thatcher: Hello Krebbel. It's a small...

and they both dissolve into laughter.

Krebbel: Took me years to find this place. I've never met a business associate here until now.

Thatcher: I have a Chock Full O'Nuts on Broadway.

Krebbel writes down the address and directions.

Krebbel: I haven't seen anything so funny since Wahl chased that car.

Thatcher: What was that? I remember hearing something about it.

Krebbel: Celia told the story about how silly Wahl looked running, looking like an agitated hippopotamus. Wahl isn't up to the weight of that job. There's no point in not telling you since you have probably figured that out for yourself.

But Wahl is as clean as a hound's tooth on that conspiracy rap. He wasn't within a mile of it. When I took over I knew I was going to have to mop up everyone who touched it. And it hasn't been easy. I had real trouble with Eberhart which the Judge helped me with. Look where that left me; practically everyone at the top level of passenger cars had to go. Jensen, our fair haired boy, turned out to be the ringleader. Holzinger and Dunn went to jail with him. When I started digging I realized we had to pressure Wheaton, in Lancasters, to retire too. Buck's backup man saw what was coming and took himself off to another job shortly after the convictions. Six months ago every single car division suffered a major shakeup.

Thatcher: That's quite a swath. You must have reached everyone in the conspiracy but wouldn't taking Jensen back undo everything?

Krebbel: There was never any question about that.

Thatcher: There was certainly a good deal of talk about it.

Krebbel: It was unavoidable. The real question was how to make his severance palatable to the Board. Until I licked that one I couldn't make a public announcement. Privately I let him know my decision. He was a last ditcher by nature. He didn't know when he was beaten.

Thatcher: Very awkward.

Krebbel: Yes, it wasn't an easy situation. For me, Ed, or poor Ray. But I want you to see that these drastic reforms make us a real potential for an excellent investment return for the Sloan.

Thatcher: Yes.

Krebbel: Wahl is a good example of what's happening here. Six months ago he was the Trucks' Assistant Manager. He was good at that job. In the normal course of events he might have become manager before he reached retirement age. That would have given him a nice boost to his pension and a little bit of glory for his last five years in harness.

Instead he's been catapulted overnight into our prestige division. He has to sell in a market totally unlike the one he is used to. I said that he's not up to the job and he isn't. But he will be. And it won't take very long. And in spirit of this kind of situation in every one of our car divisions, we've been doing very well. You know the financials for the first quarter as well as I do.

Sales in Plantagenet and Buccaneer are booming. The Lancasters are a problem, but that's true for every medium priced car in the country. Our models are going over fine this season. In another year the industry will be talking about the Big Four, not just the Big Three. And we've done it with a scrub team in the face of constant howls from the unions, government, and our own stockholders.

Thatcher: And you say Wahl is typical?

Krebbel: He's an extreme example, I admit. In the other divisions we managed to upgrade some of the middle managers. Years before they had the necessary seasoning of course.

Thatcher: It is an impressive record. But after all, your difficulties have been shared by your competitors. And they're not doing badly either.

Krebbel: Nobody was hit as hard as MM.

Thatcher: That's true. But they all had to adjust to personnel changes and to a good deal of outside criticism. Plus, of course, foregoing the very substantial advantages accruing from the conspiracy.

Krebbel frowned at the indictment.

Krebbel: I'm not sure I agree about substantial advantages. MM can do as well without price fixing. That's always been my position. If we had all the facts, it may have cost us something to play that game during the last couple of years.

Thatcher: That may be so. Basically I wonder if six months is long enough to judge the effectiveness of ... er ... unseasoned management. The momentum of your previous management may be carrying you along. It might be the booster effect of a good year for the consumer that's kept your sales growing. You can't tell what's going to happen in the next six months. Particularly when you have a murder thrown in the mix.

Krebbel dissented with a thin note of stubbornness.

Krebbel: I don't agree. Except about the murder of course. The results there are unpredictable. We're having a board meeting next week, you know. And I'm pretty sure that we'll decide to defer the new issue. With the market sliding this isn't a good time to raise money under any circumstances. But this is only a temporary delay. It has nothing to do with basic conditions here. We'll be calling you again ... and soon.

Thatcher: You think the murder will only be a temporary embarrassment?

Krebbel: Of course. That unfortunate delay in firing Jensen confused everybody. Just because he was hanging around the company people think he was still involved with it. That's nonsense. He ceased to be part of MM when the DOJ indicted him. None of our people had anything to gain or lose by his murder.

Thatcher: Are you sure you are being realistic? After all Jensen could have given the DOJ a lot of information. There must be MM people who would have suffered if he had made more disclosures.

Krebbel: The people who could have been hurt by Jensen have been dealt with. We have nothing more to hide.

Thatcher looks at Krebbel questioningly.

Thatcher: It's an interesting situation. One tends to forget that while a good many people were damaged by the trial, others benefited didn't they? On the basis of what you've said, you can see that there have been several unexpected promotions.

At this point Krebbel cut in severely.

Krebbel: That's not a view we encourage. And I wish I could convince you of that. I know you're concerned about the effects of the murder. And I've admitted it is an unpredictable factor. But remember we are in the full blaze of publicity now. Tomorrow it will start dying down; then things will come back into proportion.

Thatcher: Tomorrow? What's happening tomorrow?

Krebbel: Jensen's funeral. Didn't you know? The police have finally released the body.

Thatcher: Oh. I had been hoping to meet with your treasurer tomorrow and review your revolving loan agreement.

Krebbel: I'm afraid not. He'll be at the funeral. Most of us will be out for the day. I was going to suggest that you go out to Ann Arbor with Madsen.

Thatcher: Ann Arbor?

Krebbel: Yes. They are holding a colloquium this year on the car industry. MM's turn is tomorrow, but because of Jensen's funeral French and I have to renege. We are in something of a bind.

Thatcher: You want another body, eh? Yes, I'll be glad to go if it will help.

Krebbel: Splendid. That will be a load off everybody's mind.

Scene 18-Int.-Telegraph Fuel Stop Bar & Restaurant-Day

Thatcher out loud: Back again in the Fuel Stop having breakfast. What shows how long I've been here is how everyone waves at me as a veteran, which I feel like, wounds and all.

    Grins.

Pretty slick of making sure Madsen and Wahl won't be at the interment.

    Calls Miss Corsa at the Sloan.

Miss Corsa, what is this pile of information about New York City real estate taxes, office occupancy, and the like you sent me.

Miss Corsa V.O.: Ms. Trinkam's memo explains it.

    Properly put in his place Thatcher nods off the phone. He starts reading Charlie's report.

To: JP Thatcher
From: CF Trinkam
Subject: World Trade Center

John--

Withers wants you to look at this stuff. God knows why. It's about the new World Trade Center. Couldn't make out what's on his mind. Probably some of his pals at the Downtown Lower Manhattan Association have been after him. The infighting between the Port Authority boys and the NY Real Estate Board is beginning to heat up. If you ask me they deserve each other. Charlie.

Thatcher: Walter, you deserve this call at 1 AM since your ankle saved you from all this out here.

Walter V.O.: Yes, you are on the front lines.

Thatcher: The worst of it is you are enjoying this so much.

    Walter roars with laughter.

Walter V. O.: Have yourself a good time. I do miss it. Talk to you later.

Scene 19-Int.-Seminar Table-Day

    As the funeral service was being held elsewhere, the investigation continued.

Captain William Georgeson: I want you to talk to the sister-in-law, Mrs. Burns, as soon as she's back. Gallagher is going to check up on the neighbors.

Kelly: What about Madsen?

    Smiled a big man's patient smile.

Georgeson: I talked to him yesterday. And I'll be talking to him again, don't you worry.

Riley: But why can't we go out three nights running? What's so special about three?

Price: It is not that there's anything special about three. It is just that I don't want to rush things. We have plenty of time.

Riley: How do you know how much time we have? What if I get called back to DC?

Susan gasps.

Thatcher: Yes Walter, I am keeping an eye on things at MM. And tell Brad that only the press of important Detroit business is delaying my return.

Bowman V.O.: Even Brad won't believe that.

Thatcher: Not if you or I tell him; but Miss Prettyman will have no trouble. Tell her to tell him.

Bowman V.O.: Good one, John.

Now he sighed and went back to listening to the pretentious on stage. He was between Wahl and Madsen around the conference table.

Thatcher: Madsen, do you notice how academics can never call it a car market; it must always be fancified like French cooking. And listen to this from the brochure: a fruitful interdisciplinary exploration of the social, economic, legal, and political problems raised by large scale industrial development.

He was starting to cheer up. Madsen, ever practical, had cut to the chase.

Madsen: The Ford Foundation put up the money.

Two sharp featured, dark haired women scowled at him; an old man in a green eyeshade dozed comfortably in a corner. A question was then thrown at Thatcher.

Professor: Now if I were investing, I'd be pretty interested in capital coefficients in industries where the demand is inelastic. Do you bankers ever think about that sort of thing?

Thatcher: We've discovered that if you persist in interesting yourself in capital coefficients and inelastic demand curves, you are rarely in a position to invest.

The two scowling women deepened their scowls. John smiled in return. As they sat after the meeting ended.

Madsen: Yes. I came up here when I got out of the Army. Took my undergrad work at Texas. I was doing some pretty good research when MM asked me to head up their economics section.

Thatcher: There's much to be said for industry. The academic life has a marked soporific quality.

Madsen: Mm.

Thatcher: Do you think of going back to the university now?

Madsen: I used to think I might want to teach. Now I wonder if I will get the chance.

Everyone had left. They were at the table with the bar still open. Captain Georgeson walks in.

Georgeson: Glad I caught you gentlemen. Ah, Mr. Madsen. I've been looking for you. And it is Mr. Thatcher isn't it? Just a few little things.

Madsen: What are you doing here Captain?

Georgeson: Now look here.

Thatcher: Georgeson, before the situation gets out of hand, you'd better clarify your position. On what basis are you here?

Georgeson: What basis do I need? It's Madsen's duty to help and he knows it

Thatcher interrupts them.

Thatcher: Keep quiet Madsen. Well Georgeson? If you are asking for cooperation that's one thing. If you have a warrant it is another.

Georgeson: All right, all right. So I'm asking for cooperation. I just want to ask you a few questions, Mr. Madsen.

Madsen: All you've been doing is asking me questions.

Thatcher: Let's have a drink.

They walk over to the unattended bar and each pour a drink. They calmed down.

Georgeson: Just some questions. You had a fight with Jensen last week. A big fight. You threatened him. The two of you started in here, then you spilled out into your driveway, trading punches.

Madsen: Yes. I had a little fight with Ray last week.

Georgeson: Not so little. You told him you'll kill him if he came back. Told him to leave Celia alone.

Madsen: Keep her out of this. Anyway, Ray and I tangled last Tuesday.

Georgeson: I have witnesses who say it was Wednesday, Mr. Madsen. That makes you the last person to see Jensen alive, doesn't it?

Madsen's face went white. Was it with shock, John asked himself.

Madsen: It was Tuesday. I know who your witnesses are. You mean the McKennas across the street. Well, they're mistaken. They're old and get confused about things. Ask the Singers next door. They'll tell you it was Tuesday night.

Georgeson: Good friends of yours, the Singers. Apart from your good friends can you prove it was Tuesday?

Madsen: Can you prove it was Wednesday?

Georgeson: That's what my witnesses say. Now they claim you were fighting about Jensen's wife. Well, that's that for now. We're going to check this out. We are going to check on you and Jensen's wife until we are blue. And I just hope you've been telling us the truth, for your sake.

Georgeson and the trooper leave.

Madsen: It really was Tuesday. Although I can see how you might have your doubts.

Thatcher: It is to be hoped that someone beside those Singers can testify to that effect.

Madsen: People get mixed up. And it was over a week ago.

Thatcher: Now listen, Madsen.

Madsen: Oh I could have killed Ray. If ever I hated anyone, I hated him. Whoever did it was a real benefactor. Ray was a sadist. He liked to make Celia suffer. For her sake I put up with it. But Ray pushed me a little too far.

Thatcher: Madsen, take my advice. Forget the reasons you wanted to kill Jensen. That's Georgeson's job. Let him do it. What you should do is spend some time thinking of the many reasons you couldn't have killed him.

Madsen: But I didn't do it.

Thatcher: In a real sense, *that* is quite irrelevant.

Scene 20-Int.-Detroit Club-Day

Lionel French and former President Stuart Eberhart are in the Detroit Club.

French: Yes. I think we can look forward to some peace and quiet at last.

Eberhart (65, former CEO of MM): You're easily satisfied. What if Ray implicated me in writing? It would have been just like him to keep some dynamite up his sleeve.

French: Nonsense. In the last six months, the DOJ has been over Jensen's papers with a fine tooth comb. The only danger was what he might tell them. And that could have been worrisome. He was making pretty wild threats the other day, you know.

Eberhart: Vindictive, that's what Ray was. No gratitude at all. I gave him his start. And yet the minute he got out of jail he made a dead set for me.

French: It wasn't personal Stu. He was just looking for some leverage and where better to start than with the man who gave him his start, you?

Eberhart: That's one name for blackmail, I'd say. You seem to forget it could have landed me in jail..

French: Oh I agree. I agree. But you have to admit that Jensen ate, drank, and slept MM. That's why you picked him. And that's why he went crazy. Ray would have been great in the front office.

Eberhart: He was unbalanced.

French: Perhaps that's what it takes. In any event we don't have a thing to worry about now. Riley must realize he won't get any more evidence now that Ray is gone. You'll see. Things will start to die down in a week or two.

  2 ad men stop by to give their condolences about Ray and the goings on.

French: A loss. A great loss indeed. And now Dunn has taken a job at Hughes Aircraft in LA.

After they left.

Eberhart: Was it the Krebbel interview?

French: Yes and the carrying on at Di's party. It was awful and stupid of him. Oddly enough, he seems to have some relationship with her related to MM.

Scene 21-Int.-Holzinger Living Room-Day

At the same time Dunn and Di were talking.

Dunn V.O.: Hello Di. Yes that's right. I've taken a job at Hughes Aircraft in LA. I don't know why it should come as such a surprise to you. No, of course it isn't what you planned. Do you think it is what I'd planned? Be reasonable Di. Do you think I'd do this if I had any other choice. And for heaven's sake be careful what you say. You don't know who might be listening in.

Di: You have the brains of a pea hen.

Dunn V.O.: Whose fault is this anyway? You and your smart ideas about the DOJ. I've had a bellyful. Of course I mean you handled things wrong. I never should have gotten mixed up in this. The trouble is that I let you talk me into this.

Di interrupts him again, before he continues.

You can't talk to me that way, you and that half-baked husband of yours. Why should I pull your chestnuts out of the fire now? Di? Di?

She had hung up on him.

Di: Buck, Orin is cutting his losses and running out on us.

Buck: Good riddance.

Di: Don't act that way.

Buck: What's the matter Di?

Di: It's Dunn. I may have told him too much.

Buck: Always said he was a jerk. No telling what he might do. But I wouldn't worry about his talking. Got his own skin to save. Even if he is leaving, no company likes an executive who blabs, whether about them or anyone else.

Di: You think he'll keep quiet because he's got enough of his own to hide?

Buck: Oh yes. Say Di, has it ever occurred to you that Dunn may have been the tipster?

Di: What? But he went to jail too.

Buck: It would be just like him to mess that up too. He wanted Ray's job. And the real evidence was against Ray. If Ray hadn't talked, nobody could have touched Dunn.

Di: That's absurd, Buck.

Buck: Is it? I don't think so. Sometimes you can't stay on top of these things. It would explain why he was so wild at Jensen. Naturally, if Orin had started the whole thing, he didn't expect it to backfire on him.

Di: Nonsense. Whoever informed on Jensen must have taken good care to see that it didn't backfire.

    Something in Di's voice made Buck look up quickly. Di refuses to meet his eye.

Scene 22-Int.-Rectory-Day

Mrs. Burns: It is madness, Celia. You know how people are talking. Having Glen here will just give them more to talk about.

Mrs. Jensen: I know and I no longer care.. I'm past thinking about what people will say. I've got to see Glen someplace where we can talk. I can't bear to think of him going through all of this by himself.

Mrs. Burns: People are talking about more than your private affairs. They're saying Glen murdered Ray because of you. Are you sure you won't be doing him more harm than good by his being here?

     Louise Burns leaves and Madsen comes in. Madsen is seated on the Louise Burns' sofa, very much against her wishes.

Madsen: You know, Celia, sometimes I can't help wondering if Ray started the whole thing off.

Celia: Glen, if Ray would have arranged the whole thing he would have managed to get himself off. Perhaps he unleashed something he could no longer control. Until he was on the stand, he could have thought he was going to get away with it. You remember how stunned he was when they started bringing out those photostats of his handwriting. He never dreamed that they had so much on him. Do you think…

     As he paused she asked.

What is it Glen?

Glen: It is hard to be detached. That was a hard time for Ray. You'd left him and of course he wasn't entirely normal anyway. But I could swear he had something else on his mind when the trial started. Maybe he'd gotten tired of waiting for Eberhart's job. He knew he was going to get it eventually, but he didn't seem to want to wait ten years.

Celia: You mean that maybe Ray aimed the whole thing at Eberhart?

Glen: Sure. Remember if Ray had opened up the government would have had the goods on Eberhart. What if that was what Ray originally planned? But then, when he realized that he was caught in his own trap, he shifted tactics and decided to sit tight, hoping to come out of jail with something to sell. That would explain his behavior after he got out.

Celia: You don't need any explanation for that. That's just the way he was.

Scene 23-Int.-Wahl Office-Day

Wahl: You've heard that Dunn is leaving MM

>Price nods.

Well, we will have to organize some sort of party for him. The usual thing. You'll see to it won't you?

Price: Just the division people?

Wahl: Make it the front office too. I suppose we will have to act as if he was an assistant division manager.

Price: And Miss Price, don't forget to put yourself on the invitation list.

Scene 24-Int.-DOJ Office-Day

>A group is in the DOJ Office.

Riley: No, you can take it from me Ray was not the man who tipped.

New subordinate: Well who did then?

Riley: We don't know. It came anonymously. You'll learn that most good tips do. This isn't like customs' cases where people tip for a bounty. Sometimes it is a competitor, sometimes an insider. This time it was an insider, which we know and so does the rest of the industry. Naturally it doesn't lead to very good feelings.

Subordinate: I'll bet it doesn't.

Riley: But the thing to keep in mind is that the tip was aimed at getting both the Plantagenet and Buccaneer divisions into trouble. If Jensen had been behind it, you can be sure he would have kept the data away from his division where he was the star. Furthermore, we never would have gotten his own notes on the March 15th meeting. It is a shame he was murdered.

He would have talked, you know. In the end public pressure would have kept MM from giving him what he wanted, whether it was a job, money, or both. Then he would have come to us for sheer spite. It is really a shame. A lot of information went down the drain with Ray Jensen's murder.

Subordinate: I suppose they are relieved at MM. They must realize that as much as we do.

Riley: Exactly. I wouldn't be surprised if that isn't why they murdered him. So we will never know what he might have told us.

  One of the others.

Art (40, lawyer looking): We may not know but we can make a good guess.

Julian Summers (DOJ Attorney, 45): That doesn't help any, Art. The point is that Riley, here, thinks that the whole murder may hinge on just this consideration in which case the department has a real interest in seeing that the investigation doesn't get sidetracked or bogged down because the local police don't have access to our knowledge.

Well, Riley, if you're going to explain the ins and outs of that conspiracy to the Michigan police, I wish you luck. I had the devil's own time doing it for a Michigan jury.

Riley: The police think the entire antitrust complication is irrelevant.

Art snorted.

Art: I suppose they are just passing it off as a lucky coincidence. We all know what Jensen was, ambitious, unscrupulous, and out entirely for himself. But he never offered to make a deal. He just took his sentence like a lamb and sat tight on a whole wad of figures and names. Now, you can't make me think he was doing that because of *noblesse oblige.*

Riley: They were going to wash their hands of him and he wouldn't have taken that. He would have come to us for his revenge.

Julian Summers: And very nice it would have been. But it doesn't seem impossibly difficult to explain to a layman.

Riley: Things aren't that simple.

Art: They never are at MM.

Riley: You see, there are two sides to the coin. Jensen may have been killed because of what he knew. But it is also possible he was killed because of what he was going to find out.

Several pairs of raised eyebrow invited him to continue as he did.

Jensen was trying to find out who the tipster was. The front office had been hoping to forget about that.

97

Art: It would be awkward at this late date for MM to discover it was someone who profited from our cleanup.

They nodded.

Summers: That's their problem but still part of our business. Now the way I see it I'm not going to be able to spare you from Detroit until this investigation either is concluded or deemed hopeless. We'll give it another week, at least.

Art: Quincy (Political Appointee and the big boss) won't like that. He's been hoping to send Riley out to Denver for a month now.

Summers: Yes, I know. I got another memo from him this morning reminding me that there are other industries in the country besides cars. He'll just have to learn the facts of life about operating with limited personnel.

Riley: There is one other thing, Sir. I don't know if you have heard but there's been talk of moving forward with their public offer.

Summers: I thought they'd dropped that for the time being.

Riley: Yes, they have. But in the meantime they have had a banker practically living with the front office day and night. He could know a lot.

Summers: What banker?

Riley: John Thatcher of the Sloan.

Art: Wall Street. You wouldn't get anything out of him.

Riley: I wasn't thinking of violating any professional confidences. But he must have picked up a lot of personal detail.

Art: Forget it.

Summers: I don't know about that. There might be possibilities there. But you will have to go cautiously. I think I will leave that to your discretion, bearing in mind, of course, the interests of the department. Now, Riley, you can hand over the routine surveillance to your new associate. I want you to concentrate on liaison with the State police.

Scene 25-Int.-State Police Conference Room-Day

Riley walks into the State Police Conference room. 15 minutes later Riley says.

Riley: I think you are wrong, Georgeson, absolutely wrong.

Georgeson: All right, Riley, tell me where I'm wrong. Madsen has fallen for Jensen's wife. Everyone knows it from the Holzingers and Wahls to the MM secretaries. He wanted her to divorce Jensen to marry him. She even left him before the trial. But Jensen didn't go along apparently. Now you have to admit that gave Madsen a great motive.

Riley: Yes, I admit that--

Riley is waved to silence by Georgeson's hand.

Georgeson: So Madsen has his motive. Then he admits he had a rough fight with Jensen. Probably the night Jensen was murdered.

Riley: But Jensen was killed the next day. A lot of people saw Jensen Wednesday morning, Dunn for example. And Madsen and one of his witnesses says the fight was Tuesday night.

Georgeson: The neighbors aren't so sure it wasn't Wednesday. Madsen and Jensen fight; Madsen goes after him, shoots him, manages to get the body in the Plantagenet which was sitting by the pool. It would have been a cinch for Madsen to put the body into the backseat sometime Thursday. And there you are.

Riley: The neighbors.

    Pause.

Georgeson: Name of McKenna. Good solid citizens. Respected in the community. No reason to dislike Madsen.

Riley: And 80 years old?

    Trooper enters.

Trooper: Governor's on the phone, Captain.

Georgeson: Georgeson here. Yes, Governor. Yes sir...certainly, sir.

Riley, the Governor is interested in the case. He had ties with the industry himself you know. I told him we are 95% sure Madsen did it. He's got the motive and opportunity. And Mrs. Jensen's story is so fishy it could swim. The way I see it, she ran into Madsen, and he told her he killed her husband.

Riley: Look Georgeson. You have to admit that all you've got against Madsen is motive, which I grant you, and a lot of circumstantial evidence. Sure, this Madsen Mrs. Jensen mess is a strong motive for the usual murder. But this isn't an ordinary murder. First three MM executives were convicted of price fixing; now that's important and you are overlooking it.

Georgeson: Listen Riley, I don't like that tone of voice. I'm not overlooking anything. We've checked up on Holzinger and Dunn, as well as Jensen. We've listened to everything you had to say. But big shots from other companies went to prison didn't they? They're not dead. You've got an ax to grind, I can see that.

Riley: Don't you understand? Things at MM went to hell because nobody decided what to do with these three when they got out of jail. Look, this was a company murder all the way. It was a company gun that killed Jensen. He was found on company grounds, in a company car. Half of top management wanted to get rid of him; he was a menace to Wahl who took his job; he railroaded Dunn into jail when he could have covered for him; he was shafting Holzinger. He might have been the tipster in which case half the Board of Directors would have been gunning for him too.

Georgeson: Watch your step Riley. In the first place Madsen works at MM; he had access to the gun; he could put Jensen in the car on company grounds. I can see you are a specialist with a one track mind. I don't deny all this business stuff is important. That's why the Governor keeps calling. Nine out of ten times it is liquor; but premeditated murders are about sex, money, or both. If not, I'll turn in my badge.

Oh, I admit I haven't got enough to pick Madsen up. But he did it. We've got a lot of evidence about his affair with Jensen's wife; we have witnesses to say he was around the car on Thursday.

Riley: Everyone was.

      Georgeson ignored him.

Georgeson: He had motive, opportunity, and access to the weapon. He may have had help from Celia Jensen. We'll never be able to touch her. But she knew all right, and may have helped decoy her husband.

Riley: Have you grilled her?

Georgeson: Watch your language Riley. We pulled her in for a few questions and a sweet mess she made of them. First she says she saw her husband on Friday. Then, after the lab says he was killed on Wednesday, she says she didn't see him on Friday. Finally she admits seeing Madsen.

Riley: If she knew that her husband had been killed, she wouldn't claim to have seen him on Friday, would she?

Georgeson: That's just it. She wanted to be sure to make us think she didn't know her husband was dead. So she risked that lie. She's clever. But all we need is confirmation, just one piece of hard proof. With these big business people we have to be careful. We can't bring him in and break down his story until we have more to go on.

Say we find someone who saw them together. Near the Plantagenet. That would do it. We're interviewing every single person in the plant. Or the gun. We have already searched his apartment and his car. But if we had that gun, Riley, we would have everything we want. Madsen's goose is cooked.

Riley: Would you have a case you could give to the DA?

Georgeson: With the gun, I'd have everything.

> Riley leaves.

Scene 26-Int.-Krebbel's Office-Day

> Thatcher goes in to wait for Krebbel.

Thatcher: No, no, Miss Corsa. Tell Withers I am flying back to New York tonight.

Miss Corsa V.O.: And Mr. Bowman wanted me to ask you if you think it would be advisable to schedule a special meeting of the Investment Committee tomorrow morning.

Thatcher: On Saturday morning? No, I don't think that will be necessary. You might let him know, Miss Corsa, that it is highly unlikely MM is going to proceed with its financing just now.

Miss Corsa V.O.: Yes, Mr. Thatcher.

Thatcher: Any other important messages?

Miss Corsa V.O.: I've taken care of everything, Mr. Thatcher.

Thatcher: A week wasted. I have found out more about MM underwriting in detail, but I knew what mattered before I came out here. I just stood in for Walter.

>Miss Corsa answers skeptically.

Miss Corsa V.O.: Yes, Mr. Thatcher.

>And they hang up. Krebbel walks in.

Krebbel: Sorry you are going. I'll get a copy of those reports you need.

>Thatcher was about to say not to mind, but backs off.

Miss Shaw, will you get those projected sales figures the division managers sent in? I'd like Mr. Thatcher to have a copy before he goes.

>She returns.

Can't find them.

Krebbel: Check the other offices.

Thatcher: That's quite all right. I assure you it is not necessary.

>Krebbel nods her out.

>She leaves.

>Miss Shaw erupted into the office.

Krebbel: Yes?

Miss Shaw: Mr. Madsen had it. It was in his files.

Krebbel: Good. Well just run off a copy.

Miss Shaw: And when they went to get it they found a gun. Millie said we shouldn't say anything until we checked. She called personnel and read them the serial number. It is the same gun that was stolen before Mr. Jensen was shot.

Krebbel: Yes. I don't have any other choice now. I'll have to call Georgeson.

    Georgeson arrives.

Georgeson: What is your story?

Madsen: I don't have any story. I've never seen the gun before in my life.

Georgeson: Get your coat and hat. We are leaving.

Scene 27-Sloan Investment Conference Room Int.--Day

    The Sloan investment Conference Room.

Bowman: I don't deny that MM has troubles, but they still have great potential. I understand they have the inside track on a big NASA contract. Waymark-Sims is still optimistic.

Thatcher: And Madsen's arrest?

Bowman: Madsen may have been arrested but you can't convince me he is a murderer.

Thatcher: I'm inclined to agree with you.

Bowman: The man simply isn't the type. But that's beside the point. The fact is MM will surprise you. I want to keep an eye on it.

Thatcher: Wait a minute. What's happened to Bay Vitamins? Cook sent me a report and I don't like the look of things.

Bowman: Bay Vitamins has encountered rough going, with new formidable adversaries the AMA, FDA, and others. The net result has been the Sloan's modest investment, has been growing more modest. We sold it.

I understand Berman flew out to Detroit today.

Thatcher: Only a personal trip. Walter. Arnie is a friend of Mrs. Jensen's and she's in some distress about these latest developments. His trip has nothing to do with business.

Bowman: I see. Hugh Waymark is still all for MM. I thought maybe Arnie was going to settle things.

> The meeting ends.

Scene 28-Int.Thatcher's Office-Day

Thatcher walks into his office and see an enormous report, with Everett Gabler's name. Thatcher starts to read. Buzzes Miss Corsa who comes in.

Thatcher: Why am I reading this enormous report, Miss Corsa?

Miss Corsa: I'll get Mr. Gabler for you and a newspaper for you.

Thatcher: Oh no. Sit down, Miss Corsa. I want to know why Mr. Gabler sent me this thing. There must be a reason. I don't know what it is, but I have every confidence you do.

> She protests in a dignified manner.

Miss Corsa: Really, Mr. Thatcher.

Thatcher: That won't do, Miss Corsa. I respect the high professional manner with which you discharge your duties, and I realize that most of your vast information about the Sloan is not for my ears, please don't interrupt. But simply as a time saving device, this time I am going to have to ask you to tell me what this Gabler business is all about. You do not have to reveal your sources.

Come, come, Miss Corsa.

>Pressing his advantage. Miss Corsa capitulates.

Miss Corsa: Mr. Gabler had been summoned to Mr. Withers' suite last week, it developed, during one of that executive's descents upon the bank, between stints of deep sea fishing in the Bahamas and slaloms in Zermatt. Mr. Gabler had emerged from this interview rigid with indignation and so moved, in fact, that it had been two days before the secretarial staff learned the provocation: Mr. Withers had asked Mr. Gabler to consider the possibility of Sloan employment for a youthful connection graduating from Harvard Business School in June.

Thatcher: His nephew, Bud, and I did not think much of him either.

>Miss Corsa, as was her habit, ignored what she called Mr. Thatcher's jokes.

Miss Corsa: Yes. I understand that Mr. Withers thinks he might be useful in Rails and Industrials.

Thatcher: We will let Mr. Gabler fight his own battles. A man with his experience should be able to slough this youth off onto Trinkam or try.

>Miss Corsa unbent.

Miss Corsa: Ms. Trinkam was also been with Mr. Withers. *She's* preparing a memo for your attention too, I understand. Is that all, Mr. Thatcher?

Thatcher: This will be a battle worthy of watching. The boy is a menace: self-centered, dense, ponderous, and probably unavoidable. The family has a high sense of public duty, of course. Possibly it might be wise to suggest a career in government, say the Senate, would be more worthy of his talents. After all, the concept of on the job training has expanded since my apprenticeship at the bank.

 Miss Corsa makes no comment. Thatcher eyes her.

Thatcher: I see, Miss Corsa, you met Bud.

 She controls herself and sits firmly in place. She points at the newspaper headline to shift the subject.

Thatcher out loud: MM officer Charged with Love Nest Slaying. Can't even get away from it in New York. And then photos from the arraignment.

Miss Corsa, would you get Mrs. Jensen for me?

 She did.

Mrs. Burns V.O.: Oh, Mr. Thatcher. You know they have arrested Glen for murder.

Thatcher: Yes, I was there when they did. Just calling to give your sister a boost if I can.

 Mrs. Burns gives the phone to Celia.

Mrs. Jensen: The lawyers are impossible. They started out by trying to persuade him to plead guilty on a manslaughter charge, to claim that Ray stole the gun and brought it to the fight.

Thatcher: That doesn't sound encouraging.

Mrs. Jensen: Thank goodness they have changed their minds.

Thatcher: Oh?

Mrs. Jensen: Yes, when they heard the outlines of the prosecution case at the arraignment. Apparently they feel that the shift in the murder time is a good thing for Glen.

Thatcher: You mean the police have abandoned the idea of a Wednesday night fight? I thought they were pushing that.

Mrs. Jensen: They were. But there was a fraternity party down the street on Tuesday. Three of the students went to headquarters to say they saw the fight on Tuesday. It seemed so wonderful at the time. I thought all of our troubles were over.

Thatcher: I suppose the police now claim that the murder was an aftermath of the quarrel.

Mrs. Jensen: Yes, they say Ray was shot at the Plantagenet plant on Wednesday afternoon. They'll say anything, as long as they can accuse Glen. But at least the lawyers agree now that Glen should fight every inch of the way.

Thatcher: Well this is good news. Talk to you later.

    Trinkam walks in.

Trinkam: What are you pfa-ing about John? Miss Corsa told me to come in.

Thatcher: Come in, Charlie. I warn you I am in no mood to waste time talking about Withers' nephew.

No, no. I can handle that. It is this Maryland Fund Report. They've just hired a new research chief and I want you to tell me if I'm crazy or he is.

Thatcher: You told me earlier they hired an investment officer based on tests not knowledge of finance or markets.

Trinkam: Everybody from Wall Street registered strong homicidal tendencies so they hired this nut boy from Boston. He's above average in normalcy I understand.

Thatcher: We'd better warn our people.

>Miss Corsa buzzes.

Miss Corsa V.O.: Mr. Withers is on the phone.

Thatcher: I thought he was going to Switzerland.

Hello, Brad. Fine, good...yes...yes, I'm free for dinner... What? Oh good, I'll see you both.

>Charlie was silently interrogative as John glowered at the phone.

I am dining with Brad and Waymark. You know what that means don't you? It means that eternal dunderhead Waymark has corralled Brad, who did go to Switzerland by the way, but unfortunately came back, and now Brad is convinced MM is the buy of the century.

>John clearly felt better having gotten this off his chest.

Trinkam: Yes, this was a net addition to the considerable difficulties of running the Trust and Investment divisions of the Sloan.

>Leaving on that note, Thatcher thinks Charlie is besot too with MM.

Thatcher out loud: I must admit that despite antitrust convictions, murder investigations, and executive arrests, MM is having a very good financial year.

Bowman drops in. John lifts an eyebrow; Walter takes the message.

Bowman: John, if in the general decline of the glamor stocks, MM, old, established, and with expanding appeals to buyers being burned by whiz bang outfits, then the Sloan might well profit from participation in the new issue. I have a hunch on this one.

Thatcher: Walter, when you have a hunch I listen. OK, there it is, as distasteful as I find it.

Scene 29-Int.-Larry's Steakhouse-Day

Brad was taking time at dinner.

Withers: On Monday her husband showed up at the chalet. On the chairlift she never said a word about expecting him.

Waymark shook his head sadly.

Waymark: Terrible. Still, I envy you Brad. Skiing must be great exercise. Out of the question for me with my tricky heart of course.

Withers: You know the Twin towers project 110 stories high; you know what that will do to the vacancy rate around City Hall nearby. Playing the tax edge for all its worth.

On cue Hugh remarked.

Waymark: Heard from Berman today.

Withers chimed in on key.

Withers: Oh yes? What did he have to say?

Waymark: He now expects MM to be going through with its new issue. Things are really shaking down out there since Madsen was arrested.

Thatcher: That seems natural.

Waymark: Of course everyone realizes, now, that Jensen's murder had nothing to do with the company. Just a simple case of one man after another's wife.

    Overlooking alpine chairlifts Withers piles on.

Withers: Terrible, terrible.

Waymark: MM has really been an innocent bystander. You can't hold them responsible if one of their people goes out and commits a personal crime.

Thatcher: That's exactly the kind of defense they tried in the price fixing case and much good it did them.

Waymark: Now John, you know it's not the same sort of thing at all. If an executive goes out and fixes prices, he's acting in what he believes is the company's interests, but murder, well that's something else entirely.

Thatcher: Very well. I grant that if Madsen is the murderer it is remotely possible the stock won't be affected.

Withers: What do you mean 'if'? The police have arrested him.

Thatcher: Did Arnie have anything to say about it when you spoke with him.

Waymark: Arnie said the situation was, ah, fluid.

Thatcher: So, we're just where we were four weeks ago, which doesn't make MM an ideal investment or even a good one.

Waymark: No, we've got more information now. When you went out there, all we had was the first quarter report. Well they've just shown Arnie the sales figures for April and May. Now you know Arnie's never been enthusiastic about the MM setup. But even he admits you couldn't ask for anything better. Sales are booming.

After a moment of silence and suspense, John shook his head and looked at his two companions irritably.

Thatcher: Yes, that makes a real difference.

Withers: Knew you would see it our way. The opportunity of a lifetime.

Waymark: In any event, I think you'll agree that it might be worthwhile taking another look at MM. Why don't you go back out to Detroit? They're already digging out all of their information for Arnie.

Scene 30-Int.-Thatcher's Office-Day

Back in the office.

Thatcher: When you have a moment, Miss Corsa, perhaps you could get me Mr. Berman in Detroit.

Miss Corsa: Certainly, Mr. Thatcher.

Berman V.O.: John? Waymark called today. He said you would be coming out again.

Thatcher: If the sales numbers are as good as he claims.

Berman V.O.: Oh the sales are all right.

Thatcher: Well then what's wrong?

Berman V.O.: Jensen's murder. I don't think he did it and I wouldn't be surprised if the whole thing blows up again.

Thatcher: You've been talking to Celia. Are you sure that...

    Arnie cut in.

Berman V.O.: Of course I have. It is not just that. When you get out here, I think you might want to talk to Riley. He isn't influenced by Cele.

Thatcher: Riley? The DOJ man?

Berman V.O.: Exactly. He knows more about the front office at MM than they do themselves, and he's convinced Jensen was murdered to keep him from talking.

Thatcher: He may be riding his hobby horse.

Berman V.O.: Sure. He may be. But did you know that Jensen was threatening to start a real witch hunt for whoever gave the feds the tip?

Thatcher: Ah ha. So that's the way the wind blows. It makes sense. That murder was certainly convenient for several people.

Berman V.O.: Exactly. And Madsen is one of the few people up there who didn't stand to gain or lose a thing from the trial. That's what makes Riley think everything is too pat. Anyone could have dumped that gun in Madsen's file. He was the obvious fall guy.

Thatcher: Doesn't Riley have any idea where that tip originated?

Berman V.O.: No. But he is putting his records through a sieve again. You really ought to come out and see for yourself.

Thatcher: I have no choice. Waymark and Withers between them seem to cherish an ineradicable affection for MM.

113

Arnie's moroseness made itself felt a thousand miles away,

Berman V.O.: Well the way things are going, MM will probably make a mint even if its whole management goes to the chair.

They hang up.

Thatcher: Miss Corsa, I am going to Detroit to visit MM again, a company of which you would approve. There they shoot objectionable executives.

Miss Corsa was not amused.

Scene 31-Int. Back of Car & Rectory-Day

Back of car going to the Rectory.

Berman: In a hurry to get to MM?

Thatcher: What alternatives do you suggest?

Berman: Bloomfield Hills We are having a conference John. I'd like you to be there, based on Riley and I talking the other day.

Thatcher: I see. Are you getting support from MM?

Berman: No. They are relieved the pressure is off and want to keep it that way. They could just barely get a neutral company statement out. And some of them make me sick. For example, that Holzinger woman is going around saying it is too bad but Madsen has been chasing Celia for years.

Thatcher: Is her husband saying anything.

Berman: No. He and that whole bunch.

Thatcher: What about Krebbel?

Arnie shook his head.

You know I was with Krebbel the day they found the gun. I got the distinct impression he couldn't believe Madsen guilty. After all, planting the gun in his files wouldn't have been impossibly difficult. Krebbel isn't a fool, by a long shot. I should think he would be a good man to have on your side.

Berman: You are right about Krebbel. But he isn't in a position to really help us, no matter what he thinks privately. And he's really busy these days.

Celia greets them at the door.

Celia: Arnie! Mr. Thatcher! It's wonderful of you to come. Do come in.

Riley: I'm glad you came. I've been hoping we could get together some time.

Arnie cut him off,

Berman: John is convinced Glen is innocent.

Celia: All they care about is arresting someone. It is so unfair. Dragging Glen through this, just because we want to get married. He's the last man on earth...

Thatcher: Mrs. Jensen, as long as you have brought the matter up, would you mind explaining...that is, were you actually separated from your husband?

Both Riley and Arnie looked respectful. Celia snorts.

Celia: It was impossible to be separated from Ray. I left him and was starting to think about divorce last summer. Then after he was indicted, he called me. Of course I had to stand by him during the trial, and I couldn't very well divorce him while he was in jail. But I wrote him and explained that this was all just a delay, I hadn't changed my mind. Then...

Thatcher: Yes?

Celia: I should have known better. Ray paid absolutely no attention. He came out to Lansing and said I had to come back here. It would make things look better at the company. Then I knew Glen had been right; Ray would always find some reason why I had to come back temporarily...for six months...for a year...and it would go on and on, with Ray considering nothing but how a divorce would affect his position at MM, while Glen and I got older and older. I had it out with him. I wasn't going to wait anymore. So you see, Glen didn't have any reason to kill him. *We* didn't care what Ray did, or what MM did, or what anyone else thought.

Berman: Now take it easy, Cele. No use getting so excited. This is the situation, John. Celia is convinced Glen is innocent, no don't interrupt, Cele, because she loves him. Riley and I, on the other hand, are concerned about the business side of the whole thing.

Thatcher: You mean that the motive is in the company?

Berman: That's it. We thought that by pooling our resources-- and our confidential information about MM--we might come up with something.

Thatcher: Highly unethical.

    They sputter.

No, no. Just my little joke. What do you hope to gain?

Riley: What we hope to gain is the following: evidence Georgeson and the police are not equipped to understand, that will lead to Madsen's release.

Celia: Oh, we must, we simply must.

Riley: Or a really excellent defense for Madsen. It is probably unlikely that we can get him released, but we can give his attorney--

Celia: We have retained Leo Chastens. They say he is a brilliant criminal lawyer.

Riley: But this kind of business detail isn't the sort of thing Chastens could dig up himself. When we have got our facts straight we will talk to him.

Thatcher: I see.

Riley: Now, Mr. Berman and I were discussing the conspiracy conviction. We agree that it must figure in the murder. We decided that the sensible thing to do is to review the DOJ data. So we had been interested in the car industry for a long time. The question was how to prove conspiracy. Our investigators uncovered a lot of economic information about price fixing, but the courts demand hard evidence of collusion.

Then out of the blue we got everything we wanted. On March 20th, an envelope arrived addressed to the Assistant AG at the DOJ, with a Detroit postmark of March 18th.

Berman: Whoever addressed it knows who's in charge of antitrust activities.

Riley: Yes, up at MM I know that they suspected the clerks, but the department has assumed that it was someone much more sophisticated in business. We don't know, of course...

Celia: What about tracing the typewriter? You said before the address was typed.

Riley: Officially our story is that we had no reason to trace it. But we established it was done on a coin rental in the downtown YMCA. We went even further than that. One of our men traced the photostats to a coin operated Xerox machine at the main library branch.

Celia: He certainly wasn't taking any chances.

Riley: Oh our tipster was careful alright. Anyway in the envelope were copies of your husband's handwritten notes of the March 15th meeting. It was an important meeting and lasted two days. You see they knew they were going to have to correspond with each other, at least on a minimal basis. And nowadays one of the problems in big companies is keeping incriminating documents out of their files.

You know all the classic stories such as sales managers who are instructed to burn all their correspondence with a competitor. Or the files on a proposed merger that contains answers to questions in letters that have been destroyed. Or the memos with a big circulation list where the company's lawyers get hold of all but one copy. Well the long and short of it is that Jensen and his pals decided to play it smart and work out a code that made their letters look harmless. Then everything could go into the file, and they'd keep the code at home. Jensen's notes had that code and all the names. Once we had the code, the rest was easy. And of course, we had a field day when we were able to subpoena the actual code letters in the files.

Berman: Well they had to keep some records. Tell me, Cele, what did he do when he came back from one of these meetings? What was the procedure?

Celia: Arnie, I never knew a thing about it. Ray didn't talk to me about business and we weren't close the last few years anyway. I thought they were just his ordinary business trips.

Riley: We looked into it. What happened was Jensen and Holzinger would go to one of these meetings. Then Jensen would bring back some short notes--he acted as the secretary-- and write up a memo and have it circulated.

Thatcher: But Dunn had also acted as a decoy; for instance registering under Jensen's name in New York when a meeting was taking place in Chicago.

Celia: It doesn't seem fair that he had to go to jail too. Not that I ever liked him. Orin is a cold blooded boy on the way up...

Berman: He is, but not at MM anymore. He's quit you know.

Celia: I thought he lived and breathed MM like Ray.

Riley: It was resign or be fired. Jensen was trying to get rid of him. And I gather that after the murder Dunn felt he had even less of a future at MM.

Berman: Is Buck in the same position?

Riley: Buck is in no immediate danger. He was a division manager and a very successful one at that. It made a difference. And he had a rich wife, a wife who was very active on his behalf.

Thatcher: That's one way of putting it. I interrupted you, though. What did Jensen do with these notes? After he brought them back, I mean.

Berman: Jensen had been in the habit of giving them to his secretary to be coded and transcribed. Invariably she was asked to do it at home so that no unauthorized personnel could catch sight of her work.

Riley: Naturally, we investigated Miss Price very thoroughly. We are convinced she was totally innocent.

Thatcher: Naturally.

Riley: And if Susan was the tipster I'll eat my hat.

Thatcher: Of course not. But couldn't she make a rather shrewd guess who was?

Riley: You don't understand. To Susan they were little tin gods: Jensen, Wahl, the whole bunch of them. They could do no wrong. And as for the ones she genuinely likes such as Madsen. Take Krebbel for instance.

    Riley recounted Miss Price's tribute to Krebbel's conduct in their contretemps.

Riley: Dunn's the only one she doesn't have a good word for.

Berman: That seems to be beyond all of us.

Celia: Take the current feud. Didn't you know? I ran into Audrey Wahl the other day and she said Ed and his division are at the throat of PR.

    Thatcher grinning.

Thatcher: Lincoln Hauser.

Celia: Everyone denies driving the Plantagenet to the pool.

Thatcher: I take it Jensen was killed in the car.

    Riley nodded.

Killed at Plantagenet, transported to the pool. I can see why everyone's denying responsibility for moving the car. Particularly when one of Hauser's men is already involved as the passenger on that trip. I don't suppose anyone will ever voluntarily identify himself as the driver.

Riley: I am inclined to think it was the murderer. And I'd swear, too, that it was the man who sent us the information.

Thatcher: On the whole, I tend to agree with you.

Berman: I know that things look bad for Madsen, but I am sure...

Thatcher: A lot of good that does us.

Berman: Big farewell party for Dunn tomorrow night. You can imagine what that's going to be like.

Thatcher: If we were younger and more foolhardy, we would attend it. Probably it will be awkward enough to turn into one of those situations where the truth comes out.

Berman: Well, John. That is what I thought when I accepted for both of us.

Scene 32-Int.-Dunn Party-Day

Wahl: Of course we will all miss Orin. Particularly those of us at Plantagenet who have had the privilege of working closely with him. His contribution to MM will long be remembered, and I know you join with me in saying departure is the car industry's loss and the aircraft industry's gain. In conclusion, Orin, I just want to say that we will often be thinking of you, and hope that someplace in California you will be thinking of us.

    Orin gets up, waves, and they break for the bar.

Buck: Well, I'm glad that's over. I don't mind these separation parties once they liven up, but it is hell sitting around a table looking at a division manager behind a bunch of roses.

    Thatcher nods.

Reminds me of Hawaii. Did I ever tell you what happened to Eberhart when he landed there to open the new agency?

    Mrs. Dunn's arrival interrupts.

Mrs. Dunn: You've all been splendid, simply splendid. I can't deny this has been a difficult time for us, but Orin has always said that you and Di were simply marvelous.

Buck: Oh, Orin's all right

Mrs. Dunn: Now I want you to take me to Di so I can thank her personally. I wouldn't feel right if I didn't have a chance to talk to you both. Orin and I are setting forth on a new period.

    Thatcher flees despite Buck's signal for help.

Berman: This is turning into a real celebration. And if you ask me, what they are celebrating is Madsen's arrest.

Thatcher: Not in my circle. We are celebrating setting forth on a new period of life, though we can't deny that things have been difficult.

Berman: You have been listening to that Dunn woman. Never mind her, she's a crackpot. It is those others, especially Wahl. They are only too relieved... Oh, hello, there, Stu. How are things going?

Eberhart: I'm glad you could make it, Thatcher. These occasions are always painful.

    Thatcher nodded.

Eberhart: I have seen many people come and go at MM, but I never really get used to it. Of course there are those who don't make the grade. They haven't got what it takes. Some adjustment there is necessary. But these people who change for the sake of change, who can't wait for a division to open up... There was none of that when I was a young executive. You may not know this but I came to MM in 1961. Of course the industry wasn't what it is today.

Thatcher: Nothing is the same today. Why I remember at the Sloan in the 50s.

Eberhart: Yes. Ah, you are one of the lucky ones, still at your desk. It was a sad day for me when I had to hand in my resignation. Bad health you know. But when we get to our age, it is only wise to look ahead.

Thatcher: Three sets of tennis 3 days a week keeps me in condition.

>Berman starts but is cut off by Eberhart.

Eberhart: You will find that many things you plan to do now are too darn much trouble then. Take deep sea fishing, for example. I've always gotten in a few weeks but somehow I didn't manage it this year.

>Arnie winced thinking of his avoiding jail time as Dunn nodded at them.

Dunn: Just going the rounds. I don't want to miss anybody.

Eberhart: Orin, my boy. I hope we aren't going to lose sight of you entirely. Let us hear from you. It seems as if it were only yesterday you came to us.

Dunn: It wasn't very long ago. And who would have thought in a few short years we would both be out of the company?

Eberhart: Now, now. This is no time for bitterness. Think of the future. You have your whole life ahead of you. And a great career, I'm sure.

Dunn: Well let's hope so Stu. Anyway, aircraft's the business of the future. I've got to think in terms of the long haul, you know.

>Di Holzinger joins the group.

Di Holzinger: You certainly haven't done much thinking about the short haul.

>Dunn starts nervously.

Di Holzinger: I'd like to see you for a few minutes, Orin.

Dunn: Now look, Di, this is no place... Why don't...

Di: But then, it is so hard to find you in the right place. Your maid keeps telling me you are out.

Dunn: Well, I have been pretty busy lately. And--

Di: I don't care how busy you have been. If you think you are slinking out of town without seeing me, you are insane. Now, are you going to come with me, or do I do my talking here?

Dunn: For God's sake, Di, do you have to yell?

Di: I am using normal conversational tones. And what's more, I don't have anything to be ashamed of. I'd be only too delighted to settle this right here.

Dunn: I don't know what there is to settle. So I am leaving. I have got every right to leave. In fact you ought to be able to see that I don't have a choice.

Di: I'm not talking about your leaving. I'm talking about this federal agent, this Riley, stirring everyone up, looking for the tipster. He has been out at the plant every day this week, Buck tells me. And I want to know what you have been up to.

Dunn: Di, you have got it all wrong. Come into another room and I will explain.

Di: If this is just another rigmarole.

Dunn: No, no. Just come on. But don't say anything more here.

Berman: A forceful woman.

Eberhart: Yes, she is. Tell me, did you get the impression that those two might know something about...our informer to the DOJ?

Thatcher: I don't see how one could avoid that impression.

Eberhart: I've often wondered about those two. You have to admit that it is, ah, odd.

Berman: Ohhh?

Eberhart: I have never agreed with the company decision to ignore the spy we have in our midst. That sort of thing should be Rooted Out!

Berman: Absolutely.

Eberhart: Do you gentlemen realize that it is almost certain the tip came from someone in the confidence of senior management?

> Arnie keeps his support going for more confidences.

Berman: Unbelievable.

Thatcher: But in that event you would expect it to be someone who gained something from the trial.

Eberhart: Unless it went wrong. That's what I have always wondered, you know. What I mean is that somebody might have been behind the tipping who knew a lot but not quite enough.

Thatcher: In fact a company wife?

Berman: Or a wife in collusion with somebody else?

Eberhart: That's what I was thinking.

> Arnie further baits him.

Berman: You would think that if Mrs. Holzinger wanted to collude with somebody it would be her husband.

Eberhart: No. Buck wouldn't touch this kind of thing with a ten foot pole. But it is just the sort of thing Di would think of doing. She is ambitious for him, you know, very ambitious, more so than he is in fact, I think. But she would need someone to work with, someone who had inside information and Dunn was aching for Ray's job.

Berman: But surely if Dunn were in on it, then he would have worked things out better.

Thatcher: I think what Mr. Eberhart is driving at is this. Di can plan, but doesn't have the data. Dunn has the data but can't plan. Between them they might have flubbed the whole thing.

Eberhart: Exactly right. Of course, this is all guesswork. Probably some other explanation entirely. You mustn't let this imaginative effort of mine mislead you. No doubt Di and Orin have many things to discuss. Ah, Miss Price, not leaving so soon are you?

Price: Good evening Mr. Eberhart. No I'm not leaving. Mr. Dunn brought this model of last year's Planty. He is cleaning house and it belongs to the company so I said I would take it back. I'm just going to put it in my car now.

   Krebbel joins them.

Mr. Krebbel: I thought our sales figures might fetch you, Thatcher. And I see that Dunn is trying to get you to run his errands, Miss Price. You should have told him to call a company messenger.

Price: That's all right, Mr. Krebbel. Oh, I forgot to tell Mr. Berman which Drake to put it in. I will go after him or else we will have *you* doing Mr. Dunn's errands.

Krebbel: I think Lionel was looking for you a few minutes ago, Stu. He is in the other room.

John suspects what was coming.

I heard Stu blowing off steam about Di and Dunn. There's nothing I can do to stop him but you might as well know he has a bee in his bonnet about the DOJ getting inside information.

Thatcher: I can see he might.

Krebbel: Company policy is clear. We have weeded out our trouble makes and I intend to run such a clean shop that there won't be any more material for tipsters. As for what happened in the past, I intend to forget it. And I'll see to it that everyone on the payroll does likewise.

Oh, I know Riley's been haunting the front office. He's another one who is obsessed. But the point is that's his business. It isn't mine.

Thatcher: Tell me, Krebbel, you wouldn't care to give me your personal opinion as to whether Madsen shot Jensen would you?

Krebbel: No, Thatcher, I would not.

Audrey Wahl approaches Thatcher.

It isn't true what they are saying. Ed had the job sewed up right from the minute Ray went to jail. Ray was just putting up a good bluff when he told people he was coming back. He was always a bluffer. Big on talk. But he got taken care of, all right.

Scene 33-Int.-Krebbel's Office-Day

Thatcher is about to enter Krebbel's office and sees Hauser lathered up.

Thatcher: What seems to be the matter Hauser?

Hauser: That man Wahl is a maniac. Do you know what he has done? He's distributed a memo to List C saying that all

Plantagenets, whether production or design models, are the property of the division and not to be moved without his clearance. To the List C, mind you. Why that's almost general distribution.

Berman: Well, now, that's too bad.

Hauser: Too bad? Why he is accusing us of having taken that Super Plantagenet. I tell you, I'm not going to stand for it. No one is going to scapegoat my people while I'm around.

 Krebbel steps out of his office.

Krebbel: Is there something you want, Hauser?

Hauser: Yes, there is. Have you seen this?

Krebbel: I suppose that is the one from Wahl. Yes, I've seen it. But couldn't we go into it some other time? I have Thatcher and Berman to talk to now.

Hauser: No, it can't wait. I want a countermanding memo issued this morning. This ought to be settled right here and now.

 Wahl steps in.

Wahl: If it comes to that, I'd like to settle things too.

Hauser: So you knew I'd be up here as soon as I saw this.

Wahl: No. I didn't know anything but I could hear you down the hall.

Krebbel: Come in if you must.

 Thatcher and Berman exchange themselves and decide to include themselves.

Thatcher: Splendid. We were getting a little noisy.

Krebbel doesn't like it but has to deal with his warring managers.

Wahl: I'm getting sick of this. I've got more important things to do than squabble about who drove that car around with Ray's body. So PR made a mistake. OK. I can understand that. There was a lot of confusion with changing plans at the last minute and Hauser, here, wanting to make a circus of the thing. But I'm not going to sit still while he tries to weasel out of the whole mess and put the blame on my division.

Hauser: *We* made a mistake. I like that. You were sending the car down to the pool without even letting us know. In spite of the fact that the procedure manual is quite clear on our responsibility. If Winters hadn't seen your man driving the car away, we wouldn't even have known where to send the photographers.

Wahl: That's a good story. Even I didn't know anything about the Planty being moved until I saw it stolen. And I notice you have been careful enough to get Winters out of the way.

Krebbel: Who the hell is Winters?

Wahl: He's the PR man who was driven over to the pool in the new Super Planty. Nobody else got a good look at the driver, and now Hauser has shipped Winters off to Canada or somewhere else.

Hauser: What do you mean by that?

Wahl: I mean that you made sure we couldn't ask him who gave the order for that car to be moved.

As an aside.

Berman: Didn't Riley say the police theory is that the murderer drove the car?

Thatcher: Yes, but I think that fact has eluded Hauser.

Hauser: The police asked Winters all the questions they wanted before he left.

Wahl: They don't seem to have gotten much help from him.

Hauser: What was there for him to tell them? He is new here and he didn't look at the driver closely. All he could describe was an ordinary looking man in Plantagenet overalls and a visored cap. If you'd let him take a look at everybody in your division, no doubt we would know who drove the car.

Wahl: Like hell we would. I let him look at every man we have assigned to driving. If you think I am going to close down a whole shift when we are already running behind, just so your fancy Dan can pretend to be trying to recognize someone, you are crazy.

Hauser: Ah ha. First you say I got Winters out of the way so he wouldn't be able to recognize anyone. Now you say he is in on the whole thing.

Krebbel: That's right you know. You can't have it both ways.

Wahl: Well, then, why did he send Winters off?

Hauser: I didn't send him off specially. The front office wanted someone to cover the Canadian parts procurement. He was the man who got sent.

Wahl: I suppose he just *happened* to be the man who got picked.

Hauser: For God's sake. We have had a murder in our front yard. My best people have more than enough on their hands right here.

Wahl: Very pat. And as slick a cover-up as I've ever seen.

Hauser: Cover-up is it. If you are looking for a cover-up don't look at us. You know full well the police say that Jensen was stuck in that car because it was supposed to be trucked to New York. We were the ones who stopped that and arranged for the poolside display. And, it was a magnificent idea.

Berman: He must have gotten along great with Withers and Waymark. Sticks with his ideas through thick and thin.

Thatcher: Banking didn't have enough, ah, latitude for him.

Wahl: If you are implying that it was someone at Plantagenet who was taken by surprise.

Hauser: I am not implying. I am saying it. Which division was Jensen mixed up with? Who had the most to gain getting him out of the way?

Krebbel: Now. Linc, you are just talking off the top of your head. Ed, he doesn't mean what he's--

Wahl: Why you little pipsqueak. Running around with a popgun, trying to pretend you are selling tanks. You probably held a dress rehearsal in the garage and managed to gun down Jensen through sheer incompetence. It wouldn't surprise me if your whole gang isn't running around trying to whitewash a massacre. Ask yourself a few questions. Who knew you were going to state a shooting act as the grand finale to your rodeo? Whose idea was it to take potshots into the backseat of that car?

  The battle continues.

Hauser: I'm not going to stand here and listen to this sort of thing. What kind of fools do you think we are?

Wahl: Complete ones.

  Thatcher found himself involuntarily nodding slightly before stopping.

Hauser: Oh no. I'll tell you something. Don't talk about accidents in the garage. Everyone knows Jensen was murdered with a stolen gun. Someone planned the whole thing. Jensen said he was going to track down the tipster. You were scared stiff. You are the one that got Jensen's job. And even then you couldn't have held on to it if you hadn't murdered him. Did you let Winters take a look at *you* when he was looking at the Plantagenet drivers? You drove that car yourself.

John expected Krebbel to weigh in with a firm negative.

Krebbel: That's enough. We have too much trouble to have you two hurling murder charges at each other. I led you in here so you could blow up in decent privacy. But I'm not going to have this sort of thing going on in public. I expect some disagreements among management people. There always have been and always will be. But we have gotten along for years without accusing each other of murder, and I don't see any reason to start now. Particularly now, when it is dangerous to throw this sort of thing around.

Wahl: If you think I'm going to let him get away with...

Krebbel: You are. He is too. My job is to see that we turn out cars at a profit, and we are going to do that, no matter how much you have to swallow. I'm not going to have this operation undermined because you two, or anyone else, can't stand the pace.

Wahl: Now just a minute...

Krebbel: No. I have given all the minutes to this that I plan to give. This is it, Ed.

Miss Shaw steps in hesitantly. Krebbel responds impatiently.

Krebbel: Yes, Miss Shaw?

Miss Shaw: It is Mr. Wahl's secretary. She says he has an appointment, and are you coming?

Krebbel: Me?

> Miss Price appears over Miss Shaw's shoulder.

Price: It is the union negotiation.

> kerchoo, she sneezes. Her eyes were red and watery and she clutched a handful of tissues.

> Wahl says automatically.

Wahl: God bless you.

> Pause.

Wahl: You better go home, Miss Price. Take care of that.

Price: Thank you; they're in your office.

Berman: A little union problem.

> Krebble, Wahl, and Hauser unite.

No.

Scene 34-Int.-Wahl's Office-Day

The meeting started with union demands.

A MM accountant: You have to watch him. He is a smooth operator.

Thatcher: I haven't found a union leader who wasn't. Their stock in trade. Ah holidays. This will take awhile. Arnie, I don't know why we are here.

Arnie gives his best shrug and John grins.

Krebbel: I could not go to our stockholders with your proposal.

Berman: Nice balance of interests here. Smart cookie, Krebbel. Handles them coolly unlike what we saw earlier with Wahl and Hauser, John.

Thatcher nods with respect.

Thatcher: He is demonstrating his competence, and succeeding.

Arnie nods.

Berman: Remember Madsen did the homework and plan.

Thatcher whispers to Arnie.

Thatcher: Arnie, I am thinking of the economics not emotions of murder: Krebbel and Wahl gain; Jensen and Dunn lose. Open about the Holzingers since Buck is here too. And Wahl and Krebbel are enjoying their new roles, too.

Berman: The horse-trading has begun. Remember this is Krebbel and Wahl's first time in their new roles.

Thatcher: I am focusing on it. St. Patrick's Day, March 17, why does that ring a bell?

Berman: A great holiday. Where are you going?

Thatcher: Phone call. I didn't realize that St. Patrick's Day was March 17th.

Arnie is alerted by the urgency in Thatcher's voice.

Berman: So. March 17th is St. Patrick's Day?

Pauses.

We've been in Detroit too long.

And follows Thatcher out.

Scene 35-Int.-The Open Road-Day

Arnie is alone in the room when John returns.

Thatcher: I thought the meeting was going to resume.

Berman: Yes. Well it resumed for all of two minutes. Then the MM people discovered urgent business elsewhere, so adjourned until tomorrow.

Uncerimoniously John interrupted.

Thatcher: You didn't mention that business about St. Patrick's Day, did you?

He sounded deadly serious. Briefly Berman wondered how to explain things to the Sloan.

Berman: As a matter of fact, I did. They noticed you weren't here, and I did say that you were busy calling Withers to tell him that St. Patrick's Day is on March 17th.

Thatcher: Good God!

John turns on his heel to leave quickly. Then Arnie gets up and hurries after Thatcher. He is hard put to match the older man's stride.

Berman: John, would you please explain in words of one syllable--

John ignores him, striding down an empty staircase 2 steps at a time.

Berman: Just tell me what the heck we are doing.

Thatcher sees Riley.

Thatcher: Just the man I want, Riley. We are going to need your help.

Fabian Riley looks up.

Thatcher: We have all been inexcusably slow, my friend. Has it occurred to you that St. Patrick's Day is March 17th?

Riley echoes John's words looking as blank as Arnie felt. Then with an expression of shocked consternation, he drops his notebook and hurries after Thatcher, who was already outside the building looking around for Mack and a car..

Thatcher: That blasted car has been hounding us every minute we have been here, but when you want it...oh there he is. Mack! Mack!

Mack rose to the clarion call, jumped into a car, and roars over to Thatcher and Berman.

Riley: What are you doing? Where are you going?

Thatcher: Miss Price has already left. She's probably home by now. And I think she's in danger...

Riley: You mean--

Thatcher: I do.

Riley: I'm coming with you..

Berman: What's going on here?

They ignored him.

Riley: You are going nowhere Riley. You are going to stay here and use the authority of your office to rouse the police. We will try to head him off.

136

Riley: There won't be time…

    Thatcher was already hastening into the front seat of the car now at the curb.

Thatcher: You are wasting time as it is. And endangering her life, I might add. He's driving a 1986 Viscount, black with white sidewalls.

    Mack took off; Arnie had jumped in the backseat; Riley was running back towards the lobby.

And Mack, hurry. It is literally a matter of life or death.

    Mack hit the accelerator, Arnie reached for his non-existent cigar, and the scenery on MM Road began to rush by faster and faster as they took off.

    Riley bellowed into the phone.

Riley: I don't care what Georgeson's doing. Put me through to him now.

    Georgeson's secretary had never heard Riley raise his voice, so she knew this was serious and acted accordingly.

Georgeson? Thank goodness. Listen to me. We have discovered who killed Jensen…What? No it is not Madsen, you fool. I don't care… Listen, it doesn't matter what you think…

    Meanwhile the 1986 Viscount driver drove carefully, just five miles over the legal speed limit. .

Murderer to himself: Now is the time to keep calm. Nobody really has any notion of what you're doing. It was pure coincidence, that's all. You'll have to protect yourself against having anything come of it, but at the moment you are perfectly safe, if you keep calm.

Thatcher: Mack, I thought you said this car had power.

Mack: But Mr. Thatcher. There's a stop sign--

Thatcher: Mack, there is no time for a lot of nonsense about stop signs. Is this the best way to town?

Mack: Well, we might save a few miles if we cut off onto old Route 5.

Thatcher: Do it!

Berman: John, will you please tell me...

The question was never completed. Mack had braked the car fiercely, coming to a shivering halt at a sign marked:

> Do Not Enter
> Road Under Construction

Thatcher: Back it out; back on to the expressway.

Riley: You fool. You are going to have the blood of a woman on your fat stupid hands if you don't do something now... What do you mean, 'What'? Put up road blocks; call the Detroit police... What do you mean you will look like a fool... Listen Georgeson, if you don't get moving now, I'm coming over to take you apart.

Murderer hears a siren.

Murderer: The police--why they weren't a menace to me. Must be an accident ahead. Should pull the car on to the side road in case an accident slows down traffic. No use to risk observation.

Riley: Thank you captain. License number. Oh wait I'll get it. Have to call you back.

Mack sees the traffic slow down.

Mack: We are going to be quite a while.

Thatcher: That's where you are wrong.

  John gets out of the car. Arnie opens a window and yells.

Berman: Planning to walk to Detroit?

  Then, mindful of his responsibility to Waymark-Sims, Arnie bursts out of the back seat to follow John. Mack buries his head in his hands on the steering wheel.

Riley: What do you mean you don't know the license number of that car.

Hauser: We keep several cars out there for executive use, for visitors too. I can give you this list of the numbers of all of them.

  Riley snatchs the paper from Hauser.

Hauser: Oh, now, see here.

Riley: Shut up.

  Pause.

Here are the tag numbers, Georgeson ... Yes, I said numbers ...

Murderer: As I expected. No police activity on Canal Road. The Grand Island Tollway, while time consuming, is going to be worth the detour.

Thatcher: Riley, we are at the Exxon Station at the corner of Elm and Sebago. Have you managed to get in touch with Miss Price? Oh, it is just as well, if she's not home. And the police? Thank goodness. Yes, yes, I know it is a question of time... Just come along and don't take the expressway. It is all snarled up... Yes...

Thatcher: Riley will be here in a few minutes.

Berman: Good.

Thatcher: If anything happens to that young woman it will be because we were incredibly obtuse.

Arnie muttered: Obtuse, schmobtuse, what is going on?

The 1986 Viscount driver had tossed a quarter into the automatic toll machine and sped down the Grand Island Tollway, exactly two minutes before the reluctant police contacted the toll booth keeper.

Toll booth keeper: Lots of Viscounts on the road. How would I know?

Police: Well, keep an eye out for it now, will you? Killers.

Toll booth keeper: Aha.

Murderer: Tomorrow, business as usual.

Riley picks up Thatcher and Berman.

Thatcher: Did the state police call the Detroit police?

Riley: Georgeson was getting in touch with them. But Susan doesn't appear to be home. And it is a question of time. For all we know he may be there already.

Thatcher: Take it easy. He may be stuck in traffic as we were.

Riley: If anything happens to Susan, I'll tear Georgeson apart. I only hope...now what is going on?

The gate had come down in the toll booth preventing them from moving forward. The attendant, now barricaded in terrified isolation, refused to venture out of the booth although he noticed the one in the back seat looked apathetic enough. The cars started to pile up behind them.

Riley: What's the matter.

Riley, charging out of the car towards the tollbooth keeper. The man cringed away.

Toll booth keeper: License plate...police...

Riley: License plate? Oh. Look I know that we have got one of the plates but we are not a black Viscount with whitewalls, you idiot. We are a blue Majestic.

At this moment a squad car raced up, came to a dramatic halt, and the doors burst open with two officers emerging with drawn guns.

Riley: Do you hear me? We are a blue Majestic not a Black Viscount.

One of the police gets it.

Policeman: See Al, that's right; it is not the black Viscount we want.

Riley ignoring their guns, hurries back into his car.

Riley: Get that gate up.

Toll booth keeper: 25 cents.

Riley starts the motor and shoots forward. The squad car passes the blue Majestic and outdistances Riley quickly.

The 1986 Viscount was pulling onto Grand Island Bridge, which leads into downtown Detroit.

Suddenly the twinkle of red showed in his rearview mirror. Behind him a squad car was shortening the gap between them with surprising speed. Suddenly the driver knew whom the police were pursuing. A pang of pure fright, the first he had ever experienced, shot through him. It suddenly blurred the road with a red mist; it convulsively tightened his sweating hands.

It sent the 1986 Viscount into a turn that propelled it powerfully through the restraining wires, into an arch rising from the bridge...then, with the speed of death, crashing into gas fed flames on the railroad tracks below.

Riley: That was it I guess. A blazing wreck off the bridge.

Policeman: Not a hope. The fire truck's on the way. Put the poor guy didn't have a chance.

Riley, John, and Arnie, who had pushed their way through the gathering crowd to join Riley, had heard this epitaph.

A bystander: Poor man. What a terrible way to go.

Thatcher: Worse than the gas chamber? I wonder. Yes, Arnie. Krebbel was the murderer.

Scene 36-The Rectory-Day

Maddsen: Krebbel. I still can't believe it.

John puffed cautiously. In a rare moment of indulgence he had allowed Arnie to give him a commemorative Havana.

Thatcher: Is it that hard to believe? After all, he was really the most logical suspect all along.

Price: I thought he was so nice.

Berman: Not nice. Just smart.

Thatcher: Almost smart enough to get away with it. If hadn't have been for Mr. Riley here. Because he was the one who insisted over and over again that Jensen was murdered by the tipster. And Riley has been living in the MM front office for a year. He knows much more than any of the rest of us possibly could have about the atmosphere generated there by Jensen's return. What he said deserved respect. But it also led to certain inescapable conclusions. The murderer had done two things. He was the original tipster and he had killed Jensen. And if the State Police were right, a third thing too. He had driven the Super Plantagenet from the division to the pool. Add those three and you have Krebbel.

Madsen: I still don't see it. To be honest, I always thought Wahl was the tipster.

Thatcher: We all thought that at one time or another. Probably we made the mistake of thinking Jensen in his present job not his future one. We discounted the fact he was the acknowledged heir to Eberhart. But look instead at what the tipping actually accomplished. Eberhart was forced to resign; his two obvious successors, Jensen and Holzinger, went to jail. And the Board refused to consider anyone associated with production or marketing as a presidential candidate. Viola. They were almost forced to go with their controller, Krebbel. In other words, he got the big job. If you assume Ray, Orin, or Buck was the tipster, that individual had made an incredible botch of it.

Riley: I dismissed him from the beginning. Of course, I saw how much he had gained, but it seemed impossible he could have ever acquired the data. He was so remote from the entire conspiracy.

    Riley gives Susan a slightly aggrieved look.

Price: But Fabian, how could I know? I never connected it with St. Patrick's Day.

Celia: I have never understood what St. Patrick's Day had to do with all this.

Thatcher: It is all in the timing, On March 15th the price fixers had their famous meeting. It lasted two days. On the morning of March 17th Jensen was back in his office giving his notes as usual to Miss Price for her to take home and transcribe. But that evening, things did not go as usual. Miss Price took her belongings, including a small envelope with the notes and 20 cupcakes decorated with shamrocks, out to her car and then had to dash back into the building for something else. When she re-emerged she discovered that she had mistaken the other Drake for hers. And the owner had driven off with her belongings. The next morning Krebbel returned the envelope and gave her an enormous decorated cake. But that afternoon a photostat of those notes was on its way to the DOJ.

Madsen: But didn't Ray ever find out?

Price: No. You don't understand. The trial wasn't until October. Of course we had suspicions before that. Mr. Jensen started to get worried last summer. But he had been to lots of meetings in the meantime, and he just asked me if anyone could have gotten at the notes of any meeting. Naturally I said No. I never associated the meetings with St. Patrick's Day.

Berman: It is surprising Krebbel gave you that cake. You'd think he would be afraid to stamp the occasion on your mind.

Thatcher: On the contrary. Krebbel was very clever about that. After all Miss Price was certain to tell the story. By presenting her with the outlandishly inscribed cake he riveted her attention on the exchange of pastry. No one is going to spoil a good story about cupcakes by introducing an irrelevant envelope. That's just human nature.

Celia: Ray was set to move heaven and earth finding out what happened.

Thatcher: Precisely. That of course is why he was killed. Ideally Krebbel would have liked to cut all links between Ray and MM before his jail term was up. But his appointment was very recent and he couldn't consolidate his position fast enough to do so. So there he was with Jensen threatening to unveil the tipster unless he was re-employed. Krebbel couldn't afford to have Jensen around the front office in any capacity. And he couldn't afford to have Jensen dedicating himself to a ruthless investigation. Because by then Jensen knew enough to concentrate on the March 15th meeting. So Krebbel decided to kill him.

Madsen: They had that long conference the week Ray was killed. I wonder what went on.

Thatcher: We will never know of course. But look what happened. They had their talk on Monday. On Tuesday the gun was stolen. I think Krebbel told Jensen he would be taken back as Buck was. That was only to keep him quiet. Then Krebbel took the gun and waited for a favorable opportunity. It came on Wednesday. You remember we had looked at the Super Plantagenet and been unable to find Jensen, who was somewhere in the building. Then Krebbel left us before the plant tour because he had other errands to do in the building, according to him.

We were all under the impression that the car was being trucked to New York on the following morning. It seems inescapable that Krebbel met Jensen somewhere near that car. The garage, you recall, was deserted. Somehow he induced Ray to enter the car, probably to look at something or have a private talk. There he shot him, made sure there were no fingerprints, rearranged the body on the floor so it was hidden from view, and walked off confidently expecting that no one would enter the car, except hastily loading it on a truck, until it reached New York. By that time, a good deal of confusion would have entered the picture.

Berman: Not to mention a couple hundred Arabs. Including a reigning monarch on an official state visit.

Celia: It does seem incredible.

Madsen: What makes you so sure of what Krebbel said to Ray?

Thatcher: Wahl's reactions. At the same time he promised Plantagenet to Ray he had done so to Wahl too. After the murder Krebbel always maintained that there had never been any question of taking Ray back. But before, he had temporized with Wahl, telling him a public announcement would have to be delayed because of trouble with French.

This left Wahl, in fact both Wahls, explaining Jensen's assertive confidence as a monumental bluff. That sounded very thin, and Wahl knew it. People suspected that Wahl was doing the bluffing. The result was that he blustered in public and suspected a double cross in private. He realized what he should have realized. Krebbel was a decisive man. He was perfectly capable of making it clear to Jensen beyond a shadow of a doubt that his connection with MM was over. I had the privilege of watching him handle 2 subordinates the other day. He was not a man to shilly shally around, waiting for Board approval.

Price: Then it wasn't Thursday morning that Mr. Krebbel found out the car was being presented in Detroit?

Thatcher: Yes. And what a blow that must have been. He had calculated the body would not be discovered before New York. With luck the car might even be loaded into the hold of some ship bound for the Suez. Instead of which he comes to work the next morning and finds Hauser in the midst of elaborate preparations right outside the front office. Arnie, you know, I have wondered why our early entertainment here was so badly handled, why Krebbel didn't give us a more solid business view of MM, and less insight into social feuds. Now we know why.

Berman: The man had too much on his mind.

Madsen: Yes, but what about the car? Who drove it over to the pool?

Thatcher: Krebbel. We now have proof of that.

It was this proof which had caused Georgeson's final capitulation. Winters, summoned from Canada, had been escorted to the morgue, and identified Krebbel. "That's the driver," he said.

Krebbel was in a frenzy when he heard about the Super Plantagenet. It was essential for him to delay discovery of the body long enough to obscure the time and place of the murder. Remember he had no idea where the rest of us had been during the critical period. It was Madsen's bad luck that he wandered off. What if everyone had a cast iron alibi? He had to introduce as much confusion as possible, which he did adeptly.

And certainly he had to prevent any busybody going over the car for a last minute brushing, cleaning, or just looking inside. So he acted on the spur of the moment, rushing over to Plantagenet, appearing publicly as himself, and then donning the overalls and cap. All he had to do was wait until no one was near the car. He just got in and prepared to drive off, when Winters unexpectedly hopped in the other side and he couldn't do anything about it in his driver role. He could do nothing but hope Winters did not look in the back, which he didn't.

Price: Why didn't Winters recognize him?

Celia: A junior staff member would never suspect a person in overalls of being the company president. And I must say, Frank left rapidly enough when Wahl entered the garage.

Thatcher: It turns out that Winters had never seen Krebbel except at a distance. And of course it was Krebbel who initiated the idea that Winters be sent to Canada.

Madsen: You mean that Krebbel just parked the car by the pool, sauntered off in a pair of overalls, and called it a day?

Thatcher: I suspect that Krebbel disappeared with the speed of light, whipped off the overalls in the nearest secluded spot, leaving Winters asking us if we'd seen the driver. At the same time Krebbel stuffed them in his briefcase, reappeared in the lobby to tell Arnie and me he would see us at the Chamber dinner, before stepping into his own limousine. That limousine was the key to the whole thing.

Riley: Limousine?

Thatcher: Well car anyway. Celia, you saw Krebbel drive up to Plantagenet in his Drake on Thursday. We saw him shortly thereafter in the front office, preparing to be chauffeured about in a limousine until he returned to Plantagenet the next morning. Then he arrived at the grand presentation to the Prince in his red Drake.

Riley: Well, what's wrong with that?

Thatcher: How did he get from the plant to the front office on Thursday, if he had left his Drake at the plant over a mile away, and did not pick it up until Friday morning? That was the question that finally roused Georgeson. I will say the Michigan police may be confused about the antitrust laws, and who isn't, but they are alert to everything about cars. It was simple for them to check up and discover no company car was used, and nobody admits giving Krebbel a lift. That's what stirred Georgeson into sending for Winters and seriously considering the possibility that Krebbel had moved the Super Plantagenet.

Berman: All these people are nutty on the subject of cars. Nice to see something come of it. Delighted to get back to the IRT, after that wild chase.

Thatcher: We had another clue, too. Celia told us that when Wahl chased the Plantagenet, nobody but she dared to laugh. But Krebbel told me the same story, including a vigorous and rather funny description of how Wahl looked. Quite apart from the fact Krebbel has a booming boisterous laugh that Celia wouldn't have overlooked, I am quite sure that if he had been roaring his head off, the staff would have noticed and followed his lead. But, and this is a big but, he was in the driver's seat, not audience, watching the whole thing in his rearview mirror.

Madsen: And I suppose it was Krebbel who planted the gun in my file.

Thatcher: I expect so. You were the obvious scapegoat. Particularly with Riley egging everybody on to look for a connection with the conspiracy case. Krebbel wanted a good personal motive to take the spotlight off MM. It was simple for him to plant the gun in your file cabinet, then demand a report under circumstances which would insure a public disinterment. With you arrested, he felt perfectly safe until he discovered I had been making cryptic remarks about St. Patrick's Day falling on March 17th. Then he knew that Miss Price was a danger to him, and with his customary decisiveness, he rushed off to finish her off.

Madsen: What beats me is how calm he was throughout. He was very busy but never seemed to turn a hair.

Thatcher: He was not a man to show emotion, which had stood him in good stead in the past.

Madsen: And what were Dunn and Di up to anyway?

Thatcher: I don't know; they certainly were doing their best to look as guilty as possible.

Celia: I know. Buck called to wish me well. He said Di had told him about it. When she heard Ray talk about putting pressure on MM to take him back, she thought Orin and she could play the same trick. What she was going to do was get together enough data to start another antitrust investigation. Then she was going to tell French that he had to take back Buck and Orin, or else! But Orin got cold feet, enough so that Di was afraid he might be dealing with Mr. Riley behind her back. And of course when Buck heard about it, he clamped down on her hard.

Thatcher: And does anybody know what's going to happen to Mr. Holzinger?

Arnie: French has temporarily assumed the presidency while he reviews his depleted forces. Buck was almost certain to get his division back, just on the basis of his performance and management manpower shortage, a heady brew. There is even talk of elevating Buck to CEO. Everyone does like him.

They considered you, too, Glen. Arnie told Madsen, "But they had to discard that idea. French said he might just get away with a jailbird like Buck, considering the circumstances. But he couldn't seriously recommend to the stockholders any executive who managed to go to jail for something he did not do.

Madsen: Just as well. While French is looking for people, he can get himself another tame economist. I have had enough of MM. Celia already knows my mind's made up on that. It is back to research for me. To hell with the money!

>With a twinkle in his eye.

Thatcher: Shocking to a banker.

>Pause. Then he leaned forward.

That attitude, Madsen, confirms my opinion.

>He said gently.

You were never cut out to be a Michigan Motors man.

>And they all laughed together.

>The End

Gentle Notes for the Producer & Director
1. **Expense: Second Last Scene**.

The last scene On the Road is by far potentially the most complicated and expensive to shoot. To cut down on expense stick to the fundamentals: The murderer flees in a car; he tries evasion; and crashes and burns to death. The scene can be reduced to this through stripping out conversations, participants, and live action. Since this part of the scene serves as a bridge to the explanation, the Director can simplify the final action and focus on the explanation in the Rectory, one of the rooms servicing as the background for many scenes.

2. **Sets**

Almost all are during the day inside; even those at night are inside so can be suggested by lower lighting and such scenic suggestions.

The set designs can have a few props that suggest each location: Thatcher's office compared to Krebbel's and the Rectory; similarly for the living rooms.

Efficient Shooting:

Shoot the scences in place in sequence: Thatcher's Office, Krebbel's Office, Rectory Living Room, Other Living Rooms.

3. **Secondary Characters**

Those such as the Harried mother, blanket dryer, and barmates can be given to people for fun to be seen; they can be written out; use for morale--a major actor's spouse or friend; a mother or daughter.

4. **Rhythm**

This is a conversational film with dialogue carrying the importance of the film, not requiring music or action to carry the movie. So give the characters a chance to roll along as in a play. Seek characters who interact well and move the dialogue in ways they feel comfortable. Nuance, wit, and humor are important. This is an intelligent firm and will be helped by educated but not pretentious actors.

5. **6 Basic Scene Groups**

You can differentiate between the subsets by a few props or you can invest in more elaborate sets. Below we have divided the scenes into 6 basic groups. If you wish for further differentiation do so by props to save money; you can always do so more elaborately.

Office Setups: Scenes 1-4, 7-9, 11-12, 14, 19-20, 22-28, 30-36

    Investment Committee-1, 27

    Thatcher's Office-2, 7, 28, 30

    Krebbel's Office-3, 8, 11-12, 26, 33

    Jensen's Old Office (Wahl's)-4

    Detroit Bank's Office-9

    Rectory-14, 22, 31, 36

    Seminar Table-19

    Detroit Club-20

    Wahl-23, 34

    DOJ-24

    Police-25

    Dunn's Party-32

Living Rooms: Scenes 5-6, 16, 21

    Dunn's Living Room-5

    Holzinger's Living Room-6, 16, 21

MM Lobby: Scenes-10

Bar/Restaurants: Scenes 13, 17-18, 29

    Telegraph Motel/Fuel House-13, 18

    Diner-17

    Larry's Steakhouse-29

Laundromat: Scene-15

Outside Open Road: Scene-35

If you wish to perform this screenplay please seek permission and make payment at simplymedia2@gmail.com. Please provide your details so we can provide payment amounts and details. Many thanks from all of us at Simply Media. Emma Lathen audio, eBook, and films are available at most major online retailers and provides such as Google, Amazon, Apple, Walmart.com, and others.

Made in the USA
Monee, IL
16 September 2020